Chapter 1: The New Boss

The sound of the suppressed gunshot was sharp, wet, and final. It didn't boom like Arthur's pistol; it sliced. Scarlett watched the young passerby—the boy who had shouted in her defense—slump instantly, his cheap, plastic headphones falling onto the slick London pavement. The sudden, absolute finality of his death snapped the last thread of her resistance. Her mind screamed in silent, visceral pain, but her body went instantly rigid, her hands flying from her switchblade to clamp over her thirty-seven-week bump. The mercenary, who had been twisting her arm moments ago, froze, recognizing the shift. She was no longer fighting for herself; she was fighting for the baby.

"Arthur… he's going to kill you for that," she whispered, the threat a desperate prayer. Her breathing was ragged, shallow gasps of terror.

The two flanking thugs advanced, their movements now shockingly careful. They didn't drag her. They placed their hands lightly under her elbows and escorted her, lifting her carefully over the small step and into the massive, dark void of the Mercedes Vito van. The contrast was sickening: one moment, they were executing a stranger; the next, they were treating her like priceless, fragile cargo. They guided her onto a clean, bench-style seat, gently fastening a padded seat belt across her chest and stomach. Then, they brought forward a steel bar anchored to the floor and secured a handcuff around one of her wrists, locking her carefully in place. Her safety, her comfort, was paramount—not out of kindness, but out of necessity for the valuable asset she carried.

Gary climbed into the van after the mercenaries secured her, pulling the heavy sliding door shut with a muffled *thunk* that sealed them inside. He didn't sit. He stood, holding onto a roof handle, swaying precariously as the driver immediately accelerated, throwing the van into sharp turns to navigate and escape London traffic as fast as possible. Gary was forced to brace himself constantly, his malignant satisfaction battling the instability of the ride as he surveyed his prize.

The Confrontation

Scarlett leaned her head back against the seat, the remnants of the adrenaline turning quickly to poison. The van's interior was clean, silent, and smelled faintly of leather and stale cigarettes. She looked at Gary, the man who had ordered the murder of an innocent stranger, the man who now held her entire future.

"You're a fucking cunt," Scarlett stated, the phrase flat and cold, utterly devoid of emotion. She met his gaze, refusing to let him see the fear that was churning in her gut.

Gary merely chuckled, adjusting his stance. "Language, lawyer. And inefficient. You should have cooperated immediately. This is not how we treat our assets. But that, my dear, was entirely your fault. Collateral damage is a necessary expense when the asset is non-compliant. The nipper's death is on your conscience, not mine."

"He was trying to help," she choked out. "He was just a kid."

"And now he's an example," Gary said easily, the indifference chilling. "A necessary punctuation mark. You forced my men to deploy lethal force in a public area. That's bad for business. Your fault."

He let the silence hang for a moment, then looked at her stomach, his gaze lingering, cold and possessive. A cruel smile touched his lips, and he adopted a tone of mock concern designed purely to inflict maximum psychological pain.

"That child, that complication—I'm a traditional man, Scarlett. I believe in family. But after the way young Michael behaved in the cells... rough lad. We worry about paternity. It's a risk we need to mitigate. It's not that brute Michael's bairn, is it?"

The calculated insinuation hit her like a fresh physical blow, shattering her composure more effectively than any baton. All the shock and fear focused into absolute, burning rage, cutting through the residual terror.

"It's fucking AJ's, you disgusting prick," Scarlett snapped, throwing the words at him with venom, instantly confirming her absolute loyalty and commitment.

Gary's smile widened, satisfied. The test was over. "Good. Now we know what we are protecting, and more importantly, what we are leveraged against. That settles the emotional parameters."

The New Mission

"Now, let's talk about the next step in your career," Gary continued, his voice shifting to the calm, controlled rhythm of a network commander. "Because your value to me, Scarlett, isn't about being a fugitive. It's about being a weapon. Your value lies in the data you saw, the backdoors you exploited, and the legal knowledge you possess. I cannot risk another financial analyst or hacker replicating your moves."

He planted his feet firmly as the van sped onto the motorway. "I want you to lock down every single file Arthur ever saw. I want you to make sure no other specialist or corrupt cop can ever copy your success in dismantling my affairs. And then, I need you to redirect that extraordinary talent. The government needs hacking. My competitors need bankrupting. You will do it all for me. You will work for the bassline."

Scarlett stared at the floor, processing the magnitude of his demands. "And if I say no?"

"Then we treat the bairn like any other piece of high-value, temporary collateral," Gary said, the threat delivered softly, clinically. "The birth is a liability; it's a window of opportunity. We need to ensure the product, and its future, are viable."

The van hit a pothole, jolting her against the seatbelt. Scarlett closed her eyes, feeling the cold weight of the handcuff and the crushing reality of his demands. Arthur was chasing a ghost; she was driving straight into the heart of the network—and her new mission was to dismantle it from within, or risk losing her child.

The long drive was just beginning. The bassline had made its final, terrifying demand.

Chapter 2: The Converse Trail

The world outside the unmarked Metropolitan Police transport vehicle was a smear of late-afternoon motorway traffic. Hours had passed since the Converse dot, their only viable trace, had vanished deep into the country. Arthur was not driving; he was strapped into the passenger seat, operating as the tactical lead, his eyes fixed solely on the digital map that filled the unit's hardened laptop screen.

His shoulder, though healed and functional, was tight with the tension of the chase. But the physical pain was negligible compared to the cold, paralyzing fury and guilt that consumed him. He had seen the entire capture unfold in low resolution, watching his protective measures fail, and he had confirmed the fatal flaw: She had used his own trust as a shield for her recklessness. He was miles away, securing a perimeter in Manchester for a regional supply run, while she was gambling their son's life in London for what amounted to designer baby clothes.

"Status, Dee?" Arthur dictated, his voice flat and heavy, layered over the low static of the secure comms line.

Deedee, leading the two unmarked AFO vans behind them, responded instantly. "*We're clean, Arthur. No local assets have pinged us. We're running outside the established corruption grid. We have three minutes to the M25 interchange.*"

"They're heading for a final extraction point, not an interrogation site," Arthur surmised, tracing the last trajectory. "The van is moving too fast and too far out of London. Gary is consolidating his assets for a permanent move."

The Converse dot, after hours of relentless, high-speed travel, was now slowing. The signal was strong, settling into a specific coastal region a few hours east of London—a vast area dominated by docks, derelict warehouses, and a visible lack of municipal infrastructure. It was a ghost town of industry, matching the aesthetic of decay and poverty Gary favored.

The Destination: Final Extraction

"Pull up the satellite imagery of the final lock-on point," Arthur commanded the analyst running the digital overlay. "Cross-reference against known historical OCG smuggling routes and defunct industrial zoning."

The screen flickered, replacing the motorway map with a mosaic of grey concrete and stagnant water. They were targeting an area near a major commercial port—not the clean, active side, but the abandoned periphery: miles of crumbling quay walls, boarded-up fish processing plants, and vast, empty storage facilities that had seen better decades.

"This is it," Arthur stated, the realization a cold comfort. "He's putting her in a container, or he's putting her in a final holding cell before a non-ANPR transfer. Either way, our window is closing."

He finally looked away from the screen. *She risked Logan for cashmere booties. I'm going to kill Gary, and then I'm going to have a very long conversation with my pregnant fiancée.*

"We execute Phase Delta on approach. Zero lights, zero comms. We establish a static perimeter and rely on thermal signature only. We go in silent and fast."

Internal Reckoning

The internal monologue was a savage self-indictment. *She used my trust as a tool.* Gary had exploited the media narrative Arthur himself had failed to neutralize, but Scarlett had *given* him the opportunity.

He thought of the pain in her eyes when she had been forced to leave the young man dying on the pavement, and the agonizing finality of the screens turning black. He thought of her current state—pregnant, violated, and now facing Gary's direct psychological assault. His fury was a controlled fire, transforming his guilt into a lethal, surgical focus.

"Contact Deedee," Arthur ordered, resting his hand near the holster of the unit-issue sidearm he now carried. "Tell her we are ten minutes out from the drop zone. Tell her to prep the surveillance drone. I want every single breach point and access route logged before we set foot on that ground."

The car, now moving off the motorway and onto a rougher service road, plunged into a tunnel of dark, leafless trees. The stench of stagnant water and industrial waste seeped into the cabin. They were out of sight of the public and into Gary's domain. The tiny green dot on the screen, the Converse tracker, was now his entire world.

"We bring her home," he whispered, a promise made not to the unit, but to the woman who was fighting for their future. "No matter the cost."

Chapter 3: The Asset's Value

The abrupt halt of the van nearly threw Scarlett from the bench. She felt the vehicle shudder as the driver killed the engine. The air that seeped through the cracks in the door was cold, metallic, and carried the heavy scent of brine and industrial diesel—a dockyard. Her heart hammered a useless, panicked rhythm against the steel bar securing her wrist.

The sliding door was wrenched open, plunging the rear of the van into a cold, artificial light cast by floodlights. Gary was gone. In his place stood a new, fresh contingent of three massive mercenaries. These men were silent, their faces masked by professional indifference.

"Out, Miss Harper," one instructed, his voice flat. "Move slow, or we move you."

Scarlett was unclipped, the seatbelt and handcuff released with swift, cold efficiency. They guided her across the rough concrete apron, the *tap-tap-tap* of her battered Converse—still on her feet—sounding ridiculously loud. They entered a vast, echoing warehouse—a space clearly used for heavy lifting and cargo storage. It was here the psychological assault began.

The Inventory

"Strip," the lead merc commanded, his eyes scanning the space, not Scarlett.

She met his gaze, the terror momentarily yielding to rage. "How about you go fuck yourself," she challenged, her voice low.

The lead merc advanced one step, his voice snapping with immediate menace. "Either you do it or I do. We don't have time."

Scarlett slowly removed her clothes, suddenly very aware of the amount of eyes on her. She instantly assumed the worst but continued to remove each bit of clothing until she was stood completely naked and bruised under the cold, halogen light. She was wearing the expensive, comfortable maternity clothes she wore as a camolague only hours earlier. Her mind raced: *This is worse than a beating. This is pure inventory.*

Then the jeers started. "Being up the duff has done wonders for her tits," the man closest to her snarled, a few wolf whistles coming from others. "Jacobs is a selfish prick for keeping those tits and arse to himself," another said.

Scarlett felt a cold dread settle in her stomach. *They know his name. They know Arthur's code of secrecy, his life. Were these the squaddies he ran with? Were these the men who used to rely on him before his cover dissolved?*

Ignoring the explicit degradation, Scarlett stood unwavered, arms rigid at her sides, refusing to show them the panic or the humiliation that was churning in her gut.

A Change of Clothes

The lead merc sighed, tossing a pile of clean, folded clothing and a pair of rubber sandals toward her feet. "Put these on," he demanded, adding a layer of functional humiliation to the exchange.

Scarlett grabbed the clothes gratefully. The materials were expensive, dark, and utterly unforgiving. The black stretch trousers strained fiercely over her bump, and the fine-knit black top was pulled skin-tight. She quickly shoved her feet into the Crocs.

The clothes felt like a second skin—too tight, too revealing, but clean and warm. They confirmed the duality of her position: She was treated with clinical care, but her body was completely public property.

The Final Destination

They led Scarlett out of the warehouse, her mind still reeling from the sudden psychological whiplash. The destination was not another concrete cell, but a dazzling, multi-deck super-yacht moored silently beneath the floodlights. It was spectacular—a visible statement of wealth that jarred violently with the derelict surroundings.

As she was led up the polished teak gangway, her eyes briefly caught the sleek, silver hardware on the main cabin door—an ornate, almost imperceptible engraving: MH.

"Where the hell are you taking me?" Scarlett demanded, the sheer absurdity of the luxury fueling a fresh wave of anger.

The leader opened a lavishly appointed cabin door—rich velvet upholstery, polished mahogany, and a king-sized bed. "Your destination is France, lawyer. Somewhere your copper friend will never think to look."

She was shoved inside. The door slammed shut with a quiet, expensive finality, and the deadbolt slid home. Scarlett was locked in a gilded cage, miles away from Arthur, speeding toward a future she could not predict, but that felt chillingly familiar.

Chapter 4: The Empty Target

The world outside the unmarked Metropolitan Police transport vehicle was a smear of cold, damp late-afternoon air. Arthur was out instantly, the chill hitting his face. He moved with Deedee's team, operating under the assumption that Gary's people were waiting for them. The location was a nightmare: a vast, abandoned periphery near a major port, dominated by crumbling concrete, rusted steel, and the pervasive stench of stagnant water.

His shoulder, though healed and functional, was tight with the tension of the chase. But the physical pain was negligible compared to the cold, paralyzing fury and guilt that consumed him. He had seen the entire capture unfold in high resolution, watching his protective measures fail, and he had confirmed the fatal flaw: She had used his own trust as a shield for her recklessness.

"Alpha team, perimeter breach at the service entrance," Arthur dictated into the secure comms line, his voice a low, gravelly whisper. "Charlie team, take the upper fire escapes. We are homing in on the primary beacon. Expect hostile contact inside the structure."

The *primary beacon* was the Converse dot glowing faintly on his handheld tactical screen. The signal was strong, stationary, sitting deep inside the largest, darkest warehouse structure. Arthur knew Gary was playing a game, using the location to draw them into a close-quarters fight, but he had no choice. He moved at the tip of the spear, the heavy unit-issue sidearm held steady in his good hand, driven by the singular, burning need to retrieve Scarlett and the child.

The Emotional Trap

The tactical breach was fast, silent, and professional. Arthur reached the center of the warehouse, the dot on his screen pulsating brightly. He lowered his weapon, his breath catching in his throat.

In the middle of the vast, dusty concrete floor lay a small, deliberate pile of clothing: Scarlett's clothes. The clean, expensive maternity layers she had worn for the London run were neatly stacked. On top of the small pile, placed with sickening precision, were her battered black Converse.

Arthur picked up one of the Converse, feeling the worn canvas and the rubber sole that hid his precious tracker. It was a message: *We knew exactly what you were tracking. We brought you here by choice.*

He crushed the note in his hand. "Target is gone," he rasped, the words thick with failure. "The location was a decoy for extraction. They left a message."

Internal Reckoning and Time Limit

The internal monologue was a savage self-indictment. *She risked the child for designer supplies. I let her walk into a trap.* He thought of her current state—thirty-seven weeks pregnant, and now in the hands of a man who viewed her as a bargaining chip to be used up. The clock was ticking down to her due date, only three weeks away. He was terrified, furious, and consumed by a cold, absolute determination.

"Area search," he dictated, his voice sharp with renewed purpose. "Find evidence of recent vehicle movement near the quay."

He scanned the perimeter himself, finding what he needed near a sealed loading bay door—a set of recent, heavy tire tracks leading off the concrete and onto the rougher quay. Crucially, they were not standard commercial truck tracks.

"Thermal sweep of the quay," Arthur ordered. "Focus on areas near deep water berths. Look for large vessels that have recently departed."

The analyst reported back immediately: "*Two vessels pinged a departure in the last four hours, Arthur. Both private maritime assets. High speed.*"

Arthur's mind made the deduction: "A yacht. He's using a high-speed maritime asset to escape jurisdiction." The game had instantly moved to international waters.

"Deedee," Arthur stated, his voice a low, lethal promise. "Gary is moving her by sea. He's heading south into international waters to bypass the European land grid. We have issues of jurisdiction and international asset tracking. Mobilize the specialized unit. I need every intelligence asset we have on finding a yacht with the callsign *MH* near the French coast. I'm taking a team. You're going to have to step up and run the entire operation from London."

He gripped the Converse tighter. "We bring her home," he whispered. "No matter the cost."

Chapter 5: The Gilded Cage

The quiet thrum of the yacht's engines was a constant, unsettling lullaby. Scarlett spent the initial hours of the journey in a frenzied search for an escape. The cabin, for all its polished mahogany and velvet, was a sealed tomb. The large porthole was reinforced with thick, bulletproof glass, and its clamps were secured from the outside. The door, heavy and opulent, had no visible hinges from her side, and the lock was an electronic deadbolt that offered no purchase for the flimsy bobby pin she'd retrieved from her hair.

Panic, cold and sharp, threatened to overwhelm her. She slammed her fist, then her open palm, against the solid wood of the door until her hand ached. No response. No one was listening.

Defeated but not broken, Scarlett turned her attention to finding a weapon. She tore at the upholstery, hoping to find a loose spring, a sturdy piece of wood—anything. Nothing. The luxury furnishings offered no weakness. Her frustration mounted. She was a lawyer, an analyst, a hacker—not a commando. Arthur would know what to do. Arthur would find a way.

But Arthur wasn't here, and the cold knot of fear in her stomach tightened with every silent mile.

The Arrival and the Fight

The engines finally cut. The yacht settled with a gentle bob against a dock, the sudden silence more unnerving than the hum. Scarlett braced herself, moving to the door. She heard muffled French voices and the heavy footsteps of men outside. They were here.

The door hissed open, revealing two new mercs. These were older, more grizzled, and carried what looked like standard-issue French service weapons. They motioned her out.

"Where are we?" Scarlett demanded, trying to project defiance despite the tremors in her voice.

They merely grunted, ushering her onto the polished deck. The air was cold, damp, and smelled of the sea, but it wasn't the British coast. The sky was still dark, but a faint, grey light was beginning to fracture the horizon. Around them, the dock was empty, dominated by a single, massive warehouse complex that stretched into the pre-dawn gloom.

As they reached the gangway, Scarlett saw it—a sleek, black sedan with French plates, waiting. This was it. The next phase of her captivity.

A surge of pure, desperate adrenaline coursed through her. She was not going quietly. The baby shifted, a sudden, powerful kick that spurred her on.

With a primal scream, Scarlett lunged at the merc closest to her, aiming for his crotch with a knee, then attempting to elbow the other in the throat. She moved with a ferocity born of terror and maternal instinct, her pregnant body surprisingly agile despite its bulk. The mercs, caught off guard by her sudden, uncharacteristic violence, stumbled back. One let out a grunt of pain as her knee connected, but his partner recovered swiftly. He grabbed her from behind, his arms like steel bands around her waist and bump, lifting her off her feet.

She thrashed, a wild animal fighting for her child, screaming curses in English and French. "Get your hands off me! Let me go, you bastards!" Her struggles were futile against his strength, especially with her center of gravity so utterly compromised. He simply tightened his grip, ignoring her desperate blows against his forearms.

They carried her, still struggling violently, down the gangway and across the tarmac to the waiting car. She kicked and clawed, but it was useless. She was shoved into the back seat, pinned between the two mercenaries who sat on either side of her, effectively trapping her.

The New Cell

The drive was short, a mere ten minutes through empty, provincial French streets, before they pulled up to the imposing, windowless side of the massive warehouse complex. This wasn't just a dockyard; it was a compound. This was the French equivalent of the Manchester facility Arthur had raided, a mirror image of Gary's operational structure.

They led her through a nondescript side door, down a brightly lit corridor, and into a surprisingly well-appointed room. The door was heavy steel, but inside, the concrete walls were painted a pale, neutral grey.

Scarlett stopped dead, her eyes widening in horror and dawning understanding.

She finally recognized the room's true nature. This wasn't an interrogation room; it was a long-term, specialized detention cell. The rocking chair was too light, its runners hollow. The large double bed, comfortable and inviting, offered only plush pillows and a thick duvet. On the opposite wall, a large flat-screen television was mounted.

But it was the other items that stole her breath.

In the corner, meticulously placed, was a pristine Moses basket. On the wall, above a chest of plastic drawers, were two carefully hung bags: her designer shopping bags from London, still bearing the labels of high-end baby boutiques. She recognized the precise patterns of the cashmere baby grows, the tiny booties. Her heart plummeted.

She walked to the drawers, pulling one open. Inside, neatly folded, were clean, soft maternity clothes for her—loungewear, breathable fabrics—and beneath them, stacks of tiny baby clothes, all brand new. The other drawers held nappies, wipes, creams—a fully stocked nursery.

This wasn't a temporary holding cell. They were not only expecting to keep her indefinitely, but for her to have Logan here, in this meticulously prepared, luxurious prison. The horror of it chilled her to the bone. Gary wasn't just leveraging her; he was planning to build a new life for her, under his absolute control, waiting for her child to be born into this hellhole.

Chapter 6: A Shattered Nursery

The cottage was suffocatingly quiet. A sleepless week had blurred into an endless, agonizing vigil. Arthur stood in the doorway of the nursery, the only light filtering in from the grey, overcast morning outside. The room was exactly as Scarlett had left it, a vibrant explosion of pastel colors and soft fabrics. Tiny knitted blankets draped over a rocking chair, a meticulously arranged pile of miniature onesies sat on the changing table, and a mobile of felted sheep swayed gently in a non-existent breeze above the pristine cot.

He hadn't touched a thing. Each item of Scarlett's—a discarded hair tie on the dresser, her favourite worn gardening gloves tossed carelessly on the window seat—remained precisely where she'd dropped them, as if he expected her to walk in at any second, demanding to know what he was doing in her carefully curated space. The illusion was a cruel, self-inflicted torture.

Arthur ran a hand over his face, the stubble rough against his palm. His eyes were bloodshot, etched with a week of unyielding terror. Sleep had been a series of violent jolts, waking in a cold sweat, his hand reaching for her familiar, pregnant warmth beside him, only to find the empty space. Jonesy, usually a boisterous shadow, seemed to sense the crushing weight of his master's grief, lying quietly by the bedroom door, only stirring to nudge Arthur's hand when he saw him lost in thought.

Every resource, every contact, every illicit channel had been exploited. Deedee had been a formidable operational commander, coordinating a global search that stretched across Interpol, MI6, and every dark web forum Arthur had ever cultivated. But the world was silent. Gary had vanished without a trace, taking Scarlett with him.

The Unbearable Silence

The silence was the worst. He'd torn apart every lead, every whisper of Gary's network. Three days ago, they'd finally cornered one of Gary's known logistics men in a dingy East London lock-up. Arthur had gone in alone, the red haze of his rage blinding him. He'd beaten the man half to death, the blows precise, brutal, and aimed for maximum pain, not death. He'd broken ribs, split skin, and still, the man had sworn he knew nothing about a pregnant woman, only a high-value maritime transfer from a South Coast port. Arthur had stopped only when three other operatives, equally as large and determined, had dragged him away, their faces grim, knowing the raw, desperate edge he was operating on.

He stood in the nursery, the air thick with the scent of fresh paint and new baby clothes, a stark contrast to the decaying terror in his mind. He looked at the cot, the tiny sheets folded perfectly, the plush mobile. *Logan.* He hated how perfectly prepared it all was, how hopeful it had been. He hated the way it reminded him of everything he was losing.

His jaw ached, his teeth grinding. The image of Scarlett, pregnant, fighting for her life in a cold warehouse, was a constant, searing loop in his mind. The thought of Gary's hands on her, Gary's twisted games, Gary's control over their child's birth... it was too much.

A low growl tore from his throat. With a sudden, explosive surge of strength, Arthur lashed out. His foot connected with the side of the cot, a terrible, splintering crack echoing in the silent room. He grabbed the frame, the wood groaning, and with a guttural roar, ripped it from its moorings, throwing it against the far wall. The cot shattered, wood splintering, felt sheep scattering like broken dreams.

He stood amidst the wreckage, breathing heavily, his chest heaving, the raw, animalistic grief finally breaking through his control. The nursery, once a sanctuary of hope, was now a scene of utter destruction, a mirror of his internal landscape. He had nothing. No leads. No Scarlett. No hope.

Then, his phone, which had been silent for what felt like an eternity, vibrated violently in his pocket. He pulled it out, his fingers numb. The screen flashed: Darren Foote.

Foote was another senior officer, a grim, methodical man who commanded a covert intelligence unit. Arthur answered, his voice hoarse. "Foote."

"*Jacobs. We've got something. Might be Harper.*" Foote's voice was tight with urgency. "*She's been sending us messages.*"

Arthur's blood ran cold. "Messages? What kind of messages?"

"*Cryptic. Appearing on secure systems we didn't even know had backdoors, but also on the dark web, and… this is the strange one… hidden in a single pixel of an image on one of Gary's French property websites. An IP address.*"

Arthur's mind, numb moments before, snapped into razor-sharp focus. "Clever girl," he breathed, a wave of profound relief mixed with awe washing over him at her absolute defiance and ingenuity. "An IP address? Where to?"

"*It resolves to a coastal town, Jacobs. A small, industrial port on the northern coast of France. More like Calais, but further west. Le Havre. Looks like an abandoned shipping compound, similar to your Manchester raid, but much larger.*"

Hope, sharp and painful, pierced through the despair. Scarlett was alive. She was fighting. And she was giving them a chance.

"Get me a black ops team, Foote," Arthur said, his voice now dangerously calm. "And get me everything on Le Havre. Every single blueprint, every satellite image, every local law enforcement asset. I'm coming for her."

Chapter 7: The Hostage Ritual

Days blurred into a seamless, controlled loop inside the French warehouse. The luxurious cabin of the yacht now seemed a distant fantasy compared to Scarlett's new reality. The concrete cell, meticulously decorated with the double bed and rocking chair, was less a prison and more a morbidly furnished cage.

Scarlett knew her time was running out. Logan had shifted within her, engaging himself for the impending delivery. The heaviness seemed to be getting worse daily, and walking was becoming more and more laborious. Her back was in constant agony, a dull, pervasive throb that even the comfortable bed couldn't entirely erase. *She hadn't seen her feet since she stepped off the yacht,* a small, absurd internal observation that underscored her physical confinement.

Every morning, the ritual began. Her captors brought breakfast—fresh pastries and fruit juice, always placed silently on the steel food tray. They waited, their presence heavy and cold, until she was finished. Then, the door would unlock, and she would be escorted to a small, adjacent shower block.

The same man always watched her: a burly mercenary whose eyes held that chilling spark of recognition. Scarlett called him *Squaddie* in her head.

The shower itself was humiliating. She stood naked, her pregnancy making her slow and clumsy, every movement exposed to his cold, appraising stare. She tried to use the only weapon she had: conversation.

"Arthur always said the key to good intelligence was talking to the asset," Scarlett stated, forcing the words out against the rush of water. "You must have known him. You move like a British military contractor."

Silence. Just the low, perverted hum of his observation.

"He's not coming for me, is he?" She tried another angle. "He cut the cord. Said I was liability."

Silence. Nothing. Only the slow, deliberate scrutiny of her body. She finished the shower, dressing quickly in the dark, unforgiving clothes they provided.

She was then escorted to another room—a spartan cell furnished only with a heavy chair and a high-end terminal. This was her new workstation. She was made to hack.

The Digital Breadcrumb

Scarlett's initial fear of being forced into criminal activity was replaced by a cold, calculating resolve. Gary's demands were systematic: lock down the *Sterling Coast Property Group* accounts against official intervention, disrupt a competitor's digital infrastructure, and probe government finance databases for vulnerabilities.

Every command he gave her, every system she was forced to penetrate, became an opportunity. Scarlett was leaving a breadcrumb trail. Using low-level code injections and exploiting peripheral vulnerabilities, she was sneakily leaving a single, repeating IP address in every system she touched—in encrypted file metadata, on cached server logs, even hidden in the single pixel of a banner image on a competitor's website. It was the only signal she could send without triggering Gary's high-level security protocols. She knew the intelligence team at the Met—Deedee's people—had seen her original hack; she prayed that one of their analysts would spot the repeating anomaly. But so far, the line remained silent.

Scarlett's focus, however, was repeatedly broken by a basic, biological reality: the sheer frequency of her need for the toilet. She was highly pregnant, drinking plenty of water, and the stress amplified the need. After two days of having to ask for escort every hour, enduring the humiliating silence and scrutiny of the mercs watching her desperation, the arrangement changed.

The room had been altered. Her workstation was now adjacent to a small, prefabricated office with a functioning, private toilet. *Finally,* she thought, a small internal victory. *At least I can piss in privacy.* It was a ridiculous win, but it was a moment of control in a life completely governed by others.

The Final Betrayal

The work continued well into the evening. Scarlett was running a final sweep on a competitor's banking system when the heavy door to her office clicked and swung open.

She looked up, expecting the lead mercenary to escort her back to her cell for the night.

Instead, a figure stood in the doorway, impeccably dressed in a custom-tailored suit, carrying the heavy presence of money and courtroom power. He was flanked by a local French security officer.

Her breath hitched, and the name tore from her throat, raw and disbelieving. "Dad?! What the fuck are you doing here?"

Mr. Harper smoothed the lapel of his expensive jacket, his gaze cold and judgmental as it swept over the computer terminal, the security guard, and Scarlett's heavily pregnant state.

"Thousands of pounds in education," he stated, his voice a low, disappointed thunder, "and you still speak like a common thug."

Chapter 8: The Price of Permission

Arthur moved through the sterile command center, his mind miles away. He stood, his gaze fixed on the kitchen wall, but his mind was in the next room: the nursery. A week had passed since Scarlett's capture. The splintered wood of Logan's cot still lay against the far wall of the nursery, a testament to the destructive grief he had finally allowed himself. The final emotional breakdown was over. Now, only the mission remained.

Repair and Penance

Arthur started the repairs immediately, working through the remainder of the night and into the grey morning. He moved stiffly, the residual phantom pain of his old shoulder injury nagging him, but he worked with quiet, meticulous efficiency. Using salvaged tools—clamps, wood glue, and tactical tape—to repair the damage he had inflicted. This wasn't merely structural repair; it was a silent, agonizing penance. The cot was Logan's. It represented the future Scarlett was fiercely fighting for. Arthur spent the next three hours working until the cot was whole again, the lines true, the minor fractures concealed by the dark tape. When he was done, he felt a flicker of grim satisfaction. He had physically committed to the life he was risking everything to save.

Securing the Political Shield

The primary hurdle wasn't finding Gary; the IP address pinpointing the warehouse near Le Havre was solid, thanks to Scarlett's ingenuity. The hurdle was international jurisdiction and the political interference they *expected* from Gary's powerful network.

"We can't just sail into Le Havre and start breaching," Arthur stated during a secured video call with Deedee, his voice tight. "The French authorities will freeze us out, and Gary will leverage the diplomatic delay. We need a clear path for a black-ops extraction, authorized at the highest level."

Deedee looked grim. "*Gary's people are already leveraging their institutional contacts. To enter French territory armed, we need an exemption from the Prime Minister's office. A 'Code Red' sanction.*"

The next forty-eight hours were consumed by political warfare. Arthur, though remote, marshalled every scrap of influence his unit commanded. The argument was simple: Gary was a major institutional threat, his network compromised UK law enforcement at multiple levels, and the asset—Scarlett, the Counterintelligence Counsel—was privy to information that could cripple national security if compromised further. The clock was ticking until the 40-week mark, and the birth was imminent.

The pressure worked. Late Tuesday night, Deedee called back. "*It's done, Arthur. No. 10 signed the order an hour ago. We have a green light for 'Tactical Retrieval, Non-Lethal Primary' within a 48-hour window in the Le Havre area. Use it, because the second we cross international lines, we become the biggest diplomatic scandal of the decade.*"

Assembling the Arsenal and the Team

With the political shield secured, Arthur moved immediately to team selection. He needed competence and absolute, unquestioning loyalty—a rare commodity in the Met. He was building a team based not on rank, but on trust forged in crisis.

He chose friends. Men he'd bled with.

Darren Foote: Foote, the senior officer who first delivered the intel, was tasked with running Comms and Remote Intelligence (R.I.) from the Met side. He was Arthur's primary link to Deedee, ensuring no leaks occurred.

"We need boots on the ground, Arthur," Foote insisted during the mission briefing. "AFOs who know the difference between a tactical entry and an execution."

Arthur nodded. "I know who I want. I want the old guard."

He made two crucial calls outside the Met's current chain of command.

Ben and Rhys: Former Special Reconnaissance mates. They had served alongside Arthur in hostile environments for years before integrating into the Met's specialized teams four years ago. They were AFOs—Armed Firearm Officers—but their skill set was extraction and silent neutralization. Their loyalty wasn't to the badge; it was to Arthur.

"We heard you managed to dislocate your own shoulder to get out of a police van, Arthur," Rhys drawled over the secured line, a hint of dark humor in his voice. "We wouldn't miss the chance to watch you try to swim the Channel with a shotgun."

"The subject is pregnant, Rhys. Zero collateral damage," Arthur snapped back, the professionalism overriding the banter.

"Copy that, Logan Protocol activated," Ben confirmed immediately. "We're bringing the heavy kit."

The Final Move

The final preparation was a dizzying mix of tactical planning, equipment checks, and intelligence overlays. Arthur studied the Le Havre facility blueprints—a sprawling, multi-tiered warehouse complex that looked frighteningly similar to the dockyard he had just raided in Manchester. This confirmed Gary's standardized operational architecture. Deedee provided the latest satellite pass showing the MH Yacht's last known location near the French facility.

A week after Scarlett's capture, the team assembled in Dover under the cover of a massive, manufactured coastal weather alert. Deedee arrived in person to deliver the final brief, looking impossibly small against the backdrop of their armed deployment.

"You're relying on two things, Arthur," Deedee stated, handing him the latest satellite pass showing the MH Yacht's last known location near the French facility. "Your SR training, and her ingenuity. You bring her home."

Arthur looked at the small pile of baby clothes he was leaving behind in the cottage—the now-repaired cot was a fresh, visible symbol of his promise—before stepping onto the deck of the specialized coastal patrol vessel. The team was armed, prepared, and focused.

"We're crossing the Channel now," Arthur confirmed over the comms, watching the white cliffs of Dover disappear into the mist. "The clock is at 38 weeks. We have two weeks left." "Operation Ledger's Toll is live."

Chapter 9: The Ultimate Betrayal

Mr. Harper smoothed the lapel of his expensive jacket, his gaze cold and judgmental as it swept over the computer terminal, the security guard, and Scarlett's heavily pregnant state. "Thousands of pounds in education," he stated, his voice a low, disappointed thunder, "and you still speak like a common thug."

Scarlett stared at him, the shock rendering her speechless. "Dad?! What the fuck are you doing here?"

Mr. Harper stepped fully into the room, motioning to the French security guard who immediately left, closing the heavy steel door behind him. He looked around Scarlett's concrete cell—the expensive bed, the thin rug, the visible pipes.

"Gary is an animal," he declared, his composure momentarily breaking into fury. "This facility is substandard. Where is the climate control? The air filtration? You are carrying my grandson; you will not be subjected to this filth!"

Scarlett's head spun. *He authorized this. He knew.* "You... you paid for this? The yacht, the tracking... you're working with Gary?"

Mr. Harper looked at her with disdain. "Gary is a necessary tool. He provides liquidity and access. I provide him with legal protection, financial architecture, and key intelligence. My firm's success and my political standing are built on mutually beneficial *back-scratching arrangements.* I have access to every official, every celebrity, and every corporation he needs to thrive. Why else do you think Gary is so rich?"

The Gilded Threat

The revelation hit Scarlett like a physical blow, worse than any baton strike. The MH initials on the yacht. The endless stream of litigation against Deedee's unit. Her father was the ultimate institutional mole.

"And the baby," she whispered, clutching her stomach. "You knew about Logan."

"Of course I knew," he sneered. "He is the sole reason I intervened. You have proven yourself volatile, dangerous, and morally compromised by running with that disgraced copper. You will now be placed under my direct control. You will stabilize Gary's finances and then you will give birth."

A fresh wave of adrenaline, cold and pure, washed away her exhaustion. "I will not give you my child. I will not work for you."

Mr. Harper sighed, pulling out a silk handkerchief to wipe a bead of sweat from his temple. "Don't be a fool, Scarlett. I have a medical team preparing a delivery room for you within this facility. If you choose to fight me, I will simply authorize the surgical team to cut the baby out of you, leave you to bleed out here, and claim the child. You have no rights, dear. I have secured the legal framework. You will comply, or you will die."

His cold, clinical threat was absolute. Scarlett looked from the pristine white Moses basket (now visible in the corner) to the smug certainty in her father's eyes.

The Flight of the Mother

The only way out was through. Scarlett lunged at the nearest mercenary who had entered with Mr. Harper, using the strength born of pure desperation. She managed to exploit his momentary confusion, jamming her fist into his throat. As he choked, she wrestled his service pistol free.

"Arthur taught you well," Mr. Harper noted, sounding only mildly annoyed.

Scarlett shot the guard in the chest. He dropped instantly. The second guard lunged. She fired twice more, striking him down.

She raised the gun toward her father, who hadn't flinched. He simply looked at the smoking barrel pointed at his head.

"You are a mongrel bitch, Scarlett," he stated, his voice now dangerously calm, "just like your mother. You have your father's brains, but your mother's reckless, common filth."

Her finger tightened on the trigger, the rage at his contempt and his betrayal overwhelming everything. She pressed the cold barrel to his forehead—but just as she was about to execute the shot, a searing, unfamiliar cramp tore across her lower back and wrapped around her bump.

Her breath hitched. The sudden, intense pain made her vision swim. *Contraction.* The word echoed in her mind with terrifying finality. She had just had her first contraction.

Scarlett lowered the gun slightly, the immediate medical reality overriding the bloodlust. The clock had finally run out.

She stumbled backward, turning, her focus shifting entirely to escape. She fired three quick rounds into the heavy door lock, and kicked the exit open. She ran down the brightly lit corridor, firing haphazardly at the remaining compound security.

Every few minutes, another searing cramp seized her—a dull pain that quickly intensified and spread. Each one was slightly worse than the last, forcing her to stop, brace, and gasp for air.

Scarlett was cornered in a maintenance bay, the final handful of Gary's French mercs closing in on her position. As the mercs advanced, their weapons raised, a final, intense wave of pain hit her, far worse than anything before. With a sickening, unmistakable gush of warmth down her legs, her waters broke, followed immediately by the searing return of the contraction.

Her father's voice, sharp and chillingly calm, cut through the noise of the fight. "The baby is coming now! Don't damage the mother! Get a doctor here immediately!" He turned to the closest surviving mercenary, his voice dropping to a sinister grin. "Make sure the delivery suite is ready. We have a birthday to attend."

Chapter 10: The Point of Entry

The wind coming off the English Channel was a sharp, biting cold that offered no comfort. Hours had blurred into a sustained, tense grind aboard the specialized coastal patrol vessel. Arthur stood in the bow, the sea spray hitting his tactical gear, ignoring the nausea and the exhaustion that gripped the rest of the team. They were operating in the final hours of the 'Code Red' sanction granted by Number 10. Failure was not an option, especially now that the birth was imminent.

"Foote, status check," Arthur dictated into his headset.

"We're 20 minutes out from the drop zone, Arthur. Satellite confirms the heat signature of the main warehouse complex and the adjacent structure. No sign of the yacht. It pulled out immediately after transfer."

Arthur reviewed the blueprints for the hundredth time. The 38-week mark meant the operational risk was at its absolute peak. The facility was massive, but the target was clear: the Administration Block on the eastern wing—the only place large enough to house the command structure and the holding cells.

"Ben, Rhys. We hit the service access near the Administration Block. Primary objective: retrieval of the asset and the child. Secondary: neutralization of the command structure. Zero collateral damage to civilian assets or French security. We move silent until we hit resistance."

"Copy that, Logan Protocol," Rhys confirmed from the darkness behind him.

The Silent Insertion

The coastal insertion was flawless. Using inflatable fast boats, the AFO team landed silently on a desolate stretch of beach miles from the main port. The team moved with the fluid, trained economy of veterans.

They bypassed the compound's perimeter fence, which was, predictably, only secured electronically (useless without power). They moved toward the eastern wing, avoiding the sporadic, dim external lights that remained operational via a secondary, internal generator.

"Thermal signature confirms three active heat sources inside the Admin Block," Ben whispered over the comms. "Two stationary, one mobile. Likely one guard, one medical asset, and Gary."

Arthur nodded, tasting the metallic tang of adrenaline.

"Entry team, deploy," Arthur ordered.

They used a silent breaching charge on a secondary personnel door—a dull *thud* followed by a soft, controlled hiss as the door opened inwards. The air inside was warm, recycled, and carried the unmistakable hospital scent of antiseptic and bleach, confirming the existence of a medical facility nearby.

The Delivery Suite Discovery

The interior was a labyrinth of identical, drab corridors. They moved quickly and silently, following the scent and the strongest heat signatures. Arthur reached a juncture and saw a small window in a steel door, giving him a brief, horrifying glimpse inside.

He stopped dead.

Scarlett was lying on a steel-framed surgical bed, secured by leather straps at her wrists and ankles. She was pale, drenched in sweat, and looked utterly spent. Her dark hair was matted to her temples. The stark, visible stillness of her body sent a lightning bolt of cold, paralyzing fear through Arthur.

She's dead. They killed her.

"Breaching charge, now!" Arthur roared, snapping the order.

The door blew inward with a loud, violent *CRACK*. Arthur was through the smoke before the metal stopped rattling.

The room was large, sterile, and blindingly bright. A civilian doctor in surgical scrubs stood near a rolling cart, his hands raised in surrender.

Arthur moved instantly, covering the distance in two steps. He fell to his knees beside the bed, oblivious to the armed men around him. "Scarlett!" he roared, reaching out to touch her face, his voice thick with raw, visceral grief.

Then, he felt it. Beneath his frantic touch, her body seized. Her jaw clenched, her head arched back against the pillow, and a guttural, primal scream of absolute agony ripped from her throat. It was a deep, sustained contraction.

Arthur froze, the grief instantly replaced by the terrifying reality of active labor.

"Doctor, status!" Arthur roared, spinning to face the terrified man. "How far along is she? What is the status of the child?"

The doctor, hands shaking, answered immediately. "It's been eight hours since her waters broke, sir! She's only five centimeters dilated, the baby is showing distress, and if this arrest in dilation continues, she will require an emergency C-section!"

Arthur gripped her hand, his eyes burning into hers, pleading for her to stay anchored. She was in hell, and the final clock was ticking.

Chapter 11: Holding the Line

The cold dread that had seized Arthur upon hearing the doctor's assessment—five centimeters, eight hours, distress—hardened into lethal focus. He knew immediately the extraction was off. There was no moving Scarlett.

He was beside the bed in an instant, using the keys from the surrendered guard to free her wrists and ankles from the leather restraints. Her skin was raw and chafed. He gently peeled the straps away.

Scarlett's eyes, glazed over with pain and exertion, fluttered open. She saw only him, the bright lights and armed men around them irrelevant. With a surge of strength that seemed impossible, she grabbed the collar of his tactical shirt.

"Get me the fuck out of here!" she screamed, the command raw, desperate, and completely understandable.

"I can't, Scarlett," he whispered, holding her face. "You're not moving. The contractions are too fast. They're every minute."

The Demand for Drugs

The realization of the medical reality hit them both. Scarlett's focus shifted entirely to the immense, crushing pain.

"I don't care," she hissed, her eyes wild with agony. "I want all the drugs! Fuck the birth plan! I want to be higher than fucking Snoop Dogg! Get me an epidural, and if they don't have that, raid Gary's stash! I'll take anything!"

Arthur ignored the illegal and desperate plea, immediately pivoting to the doctor for available, safe relief.

"Rhys, Ben! Secure the corridor!" Arthur barked into his comms. "Foote, we're locked down! We're holding the delivery room! The asset cannot be moved!"

Arthur turned to the doctor, his eyes demanding immediate, practical information. "Forget the radio, Doctor. It's compromised. What legitimate pain relief do you have available? We need to manage the trauma now."

The doctor, Henri, stared wide-eyed at Arthur, then glanced fearfully toward the door. "Sir, I... I was given explicit instructions. When I prepared the room, I was told there would be no chemical intervention—no epidural, no strong narcotics. They demanded a 'drugless' birth."

Arthur froze, the implication immediate and sickening. "Who gave that order, Doctor? Who mandated 'drugless'?"

Henri swallowed hard. "A civilian, sir. A very powerful gentleman. Mr. Harper. He insisted. He threatened my entire medical license if I didn't comply."

The Return to Hell

Arthur absorbed the final, brutal realization: Mr. Harper was here. He was controlling the delivery. The institutional corruption was a deliberate act of vengeance, designed to make Scarlett suffer through the maximum possible pain.

"Doctor, what instruments do you need? What drugs are critical?" Arthur resumed, his voice heavy with lethal calm.

Henri began listing items. "Scalpels, clamps, sutures, local anesthetics, pitocin, blood—"

"Instruments and local drugs only," Arthur stated. "We will secure this room and assist you." He looked at Ben and Rhys. "We ran stabilization and field surgery in Kabul and Helmand for years. We know sepsis control, hemorrhage management, and trauma protocol. We will secure this room and assist you."

"Rhys, Ben! Get the surgical tools prepped and sterilized! You two are the surgical techs. I'm on hemorrhage and security."

He returned to Scarlett, whose face was now slick with tears and effort. He knew he had to deliver the final piece of the betrayal.

"Baby, baby, look at me," he murmured, gently wiping the sweat from her temple. "I know why there are no drugs, and I know who is controlling this."

Scarlett's eyes snapped open just as the room seemed to contract. A primal, immediate agony seized her body, arching her back and ripping a sound of pure pain from her chest.

"Get this fucking thing out of me!" she screamed, twisting violently, knuckles white from grasping the bars of the bed. "I hate all of you! You're all fucking monsters!" The pain consumed her, turning her fear into raw, incoherent rage directed at everyone in the room.

Arthur held her, anchoring her through the storm. The siege was no longer just external; it was inside the room, inside her body. They were locked in a fight against time, pain, and the final, brutal machinations of her own father.

Chapter 12: The Raging Heart

The sterile INFIRMERIE room instantly transformed into a battlefield command center. The raw, guttural rage Scarlett had unleashed was a tactical warning shot. Arthur knew Gary's men would already be mobilizing.

"Rhys, Ben! Barricade that corridor, now!" Arthur roared, snapping into operational mode. He grabbed the heavy surgical cart and shoved it against the steel doorframe. "Foote, what's our contact status? How many confirmed heat signatures inbound?"

"*Five active, moving fast down the central corridor, Arthur! Likely hostile! They're cutting off the secondary service route!*" Foote's voice crackled from the handheld comms unit.

Arthur ignored the incoming threat for a crucial second, focusing on the human factor. He moved back to the doctor, Henri, whose hands were shaking violently. "Doctor, you have two jobs: secure the medical equipment and prep the mother. I need a clear assessment."

Henri, galvanized by Arthur's sudden control, checked Scarlett quickly. His face, still pale, shifted to disbelief. "Sir, the dilation has suddenly accelerated! She's gone from five centimeters to eight!"

Arthur absorbed the impossible, miraculous news. He looked from the monitor to the doctor. "The trauma was locking her up. You being here seems to have made your son play ball, sir. The psychological safety released the tension."

But the battle was far from over.

The Impossible Dual Front

"Eight centimeters is not enough!" Arthur yelled, turning toward the reinforced steel door. "Rhys, fire-axes! Lock the hinges!"

A searing contraction seized Scarlett. She gripped the sheet, tears streaming, but her eyes snapped open, blazing with defiance. "I'm fucking trying! How about you push and I'll shoot the fucking gun?" she screamed, channeling her agony into the tactical situation.

Rhys, who was stacking surgical supplies near the door, suppressed a grin. He glanced at Arthur. "She's pure fighting spirit, mate. You picked a good one."

The mercenary assault began almost instantly. A volley of small arms fire slammed into the steel door, making the concrete walls vibrate. Ben and Rhys returned fire precisely, aiming for non-lethal neutralization, forcing the attackers to pull back momentarily. The air was thick with the smell of gunpowder and antiseptic.

Arthur was trapped in an impossible dual front: defending the room from external enemies while simultaneously managing the escalating crisis on the bed.

He moved to Scarlett, taking her hand. "Listen to me, Arthur," Scarlett insisted, her voice tight with renewed purpose. "Your mates are going nowhere near my fucking vagina. it's the doctor and you. They stay on the door."

"Understood, lawyer," Arthur confirmed, respecting the absolute boundary instantly. "They are security and surgical techs only."

Preparations and Breakthrough

"Doctor, the child's status! Is the distress worsening?" Arthur demanded.

Henri pointed a shaky, gloved finger at the portable fetal monitor. "The heart rate is erratic, sir. The baby is still in distress. We must maintain absolute readiness for surgery."

The siege continued with sustained intensity. The mercenaries outside the door tried breaching charges, which Ben and Rhys neutralized using fire extinguishers and suppressive fire. Arthur, ignoring the immediate battle, focused his energy entirely on Scarlett, coaching her, anchoring her, and leveraging her immense will to fight the pain.

The contractions, though agonizing, were becoming more efficient. Henri monitored her diligently, risking life and limb to remain professional amid the chaos of the besieged room.

"The pain is too much, Arthur," Scarlett pleaded, her knuckles white as she gripped the sheets. "It's too much."

"I know, baby. I know," he replied, gently supporting her back. "But remember why. Remember your father's *gift*. He wanted you broken, but you are not. Every contraction is a step away from him. You are doing this, Scarlett. You are winning this war for Logan."

His words, brutal and true, served as a potent anchor. The battle raged outside, but the biological war was reaching its climax.

Suddenly, Henri let out a sharp gasp, his eyes wide. "Sir! She's at ten centimeters!"

Arthur froze, the tactical plan dissolving instantly. The external siege was irrelevant. The internal siege was over. The extraction was no longer an option. The baby was coming now

Chapter 13: The Battlefield Birth

The world had narrowed to the bed and the steel door. Scarlett lay on the birthing bed, her body a screaming battleground where biology and terror fought for control. She was ten centimeters dilated, the point of no return. Her chest heaved, slick with sweat and effort, but the sheer, agonizing duration of the contractions was crushing her will.

"I can't, Arthur, I can't!" Scarlett screamed, the raw honesty of her failure tearing through her throat. The pain was absolute, eclipsing the gunshot wound, the torture, and the fear of the siege. It was a dense, physical fire that radiated from her spine, demanding release.

Arthur was her sole anchor. He was braced against the side of the bed, his hand a vise around hers. He was oblivious to the gunfire and the shouting outside the barricaded door; his world was contained in her face.

"You can, lawyer, you can," Arthur coached, his voice rough with emotion, yet firm with operational command. "You push like you're breaching a door! You find the target! Now! Focus that pain, Scarlett! Don't you surrender!"

She bit down on the sheet, her body convulsing with a massive contraction. She pushed with a desperate, primal bellow, focusing every ounce of her will—the will that had beaten Michael, that had survived the cell, that had dismantled Gary's finances—onto this singular, impossible task.

"Again! You hit the target! Don't let up!" Arthur commanded.

The external battle was irrelevant until it wasn't. As the final, immense wave of force seized her body, there was a deafening roar from the corridor. The makeshift barricade—the surgical cart and the fire axes—groaned under a sudden, focused assault.

The Last Shot

"We've got company! They're breaching!" Rhys yelled across slamming suppressive fire towards the door.

A second team of mercenaries, heavier and more aggressive than the first, was attempting to blast through the door. The sound of a crowbar tearing at the metal was instantaneous.

"Arthur!" Scarlett shrieked, the panic of the physical pain mixing with the terror of the invasion. "They're coming!"

Arthur's face was a mask of cold fury and pure terror. He saw the flash of an eye and a gloved hand appear in the fractured steel of the door. With a guttural snarl, he drew the unit sidearm with his good hand and fired one single, precise shot. The bullet struck true, and the noise of the assault stopped instantly, replaced by a heavy, sickening thud. He had neutralized the lead mercenary, buying them seconds.

But the action cost them. The surge of adrenaline and shock propelled her into the absolute, final stage of labor. The pain was no longer just fire; it was tearing, splitting agony.

"I can't—it's burning!" Scarlett screamed, gripping the sheets, her body bowing backward, feeling the immense pressure that could not be stopped.

"The head is crowning, Madam!" Doctor Henri yelled, his voice strained but professional, his hands already positioned. "Push hard, now! We need the head out! Now!"

Scarlett screamed—a raw, sustained sound of total physical release and searing intensity. It wasn't human language; it was the noise of creation and destruction. The pain peaked, consuming her, followed by a shocking, unbelievable sensation of tearing relief.

"It's here! The head is delivered!" Doctor Henri shouted over the lingering smoke and echoes of gunfire.

A New Life in the Ruins

Arthur, his gun still smoking, holstered it instantly. He was back at the bedside, his eyes wide, fixed on the slick, bruised infant now partially delivered. "He's here," Arthur whispered, the disbelief overwhelming his exhaustion.

Scarlett felt the final, slippery rush as the rest of the body was delivered onto the sheet. The silence was immediate and terrifying. The noise of the siege—the shouts of the remaining mercenaries, the steady return fire from Rhys and Ben—seemed distant, muted. The entire room held its breath.

The baby was silent. Completely, unnervingly silent.

Doctor Henri worked frantically, his hands efficient and quick, clearing the baby's airway. Arthur stood, utterly immobile, his eyes fixed on the limp, tiny body.

Then, a sudden, powerful, earth-shattering CRY filled the room. It wasn't the weak mewling of an infant; it was a strong, robust roar that cut through the silence of the siege, announcing life.

Tears, hot and immediate, streamed down Arthur's soot-blackened face. Scarlett watched him, stunned by the sheer depth of the emotion—the soldier who never cried was sobbing freely.

Doctor Henri cut the cord. "He's perfect, Ms. Harper! A healthy boy!"

Arthur reached for the child. He used the small, custom tactical knife Rhys had given him years ago—the same knife he used for fieldwork and survival—to cut the final tether, separating his son from his girlfriend. The action was intimate and utterly surreal. He was handed his son, a tiny, impossibly small creature barely bigger than his hand, his skin mottled and angry, but impossibly alive.

"Logan," Arthur choked out, pulling the child close to his chest, sinking onto the cold floor of the infirmary. The siege was over. The extraction had failed, but the birth was successful. They had won the war for their son.

Chapter 14: The Final Extraction

The silence that followed Logan's first cry was shattered by the renewed, urgent shouts of Arthur. He ignored the blood-soaked scene and the armed men securing the perimeter. The external fight was over; the internal fight was paramount.

Arthur leaned over the surgical bed, his face—blackened with soot and streaked with tears—a mask of pure, possessive relief. He placed the bundled, screaming infant carefully into Scarlett's arms.

"He's perfect, my love," Arthur choked out, his voice thick with a raw, unfamiliar emotion. "He's Logan. Hold him." He waited just long enough to see her battered body relax slightly as she clutched their son, anchoring herself to the small, warm life.

Arthur spun instantly to face Doctor Henri, the French GP who had just delivered the child amidst a firefight. Henri was standing over the surgical cart, his hands shaking violently.

"Doctor!" Arthur roared, the sound cutting through the tactical comms. "Get her fit to move! Now! I need immediate hemorrhage control, stabilization, and a full trauma dose for the mother. Zero narcotics, just immediate trauma management. The baby needs to be cleared for transport."

Henri, professional, nodded, pointing to the surgical table. "She lost blood, sir! I need to stabilize the uterine contractions! And the child needs immediate thermal support."

Clearing the Field and Congratulations

Arthur left the bedside only when the medical team—now consisting of Henri and Ben (who had traded his rifle for sterile gloves)—was focused entirely on Scarlett. He moved to the corridor, where Rhys was securing the final blast door.

"Status on Gary and Mr. Harper?" Arthur demanded, his eyes scanning the smoke-filled corridor.

Rhys shook his head grimly. "They're long gone, Arthur. Clean break. Gary took a round, but he'll be patched up now. Mr. Harper left the dirty work to the mercs; we found no trace of him."

Rhys lowered his rifle, walking toward Arthur. "Welcome to the club, mate. Well done, Daddy."

The congratulations immediately poured in over the comms. "*That's a strong set of lungs, Jacobs. Heard the little man over the comms static. Congrats, from all of us,*" Foote's voice crackled, laced with genuine warmth.

"Copy that, Foote. New objective is immediate Medevac," Arthur confirmed, his voice thick with the emotion of the moment. "Tell Deedee the extraction is complex. We have two critical medical assets: one severe gunshot wound, one immediate thermal support required."

The Political Gambit and Final Lift

The air was ripped apart by the heavy, rhythmic beat of rotor blades. The sound was immense, growing rapidly louder.

"Extraction is here," Rhys announced, unbarricading the exterior door. "French Air Force markings. They're clean."

Arthur looked at his son, nestled securely against Scarlett's chest, and then at the exhausted woman who had just won the most brutal fight of her life.

"Hold on, my heart," he murmured, kissing her forehead.

He moved with painstaking care, supporting Scarlett against his chest, ensuring the newborn was secured safely against his mother. He bypassed the stretcher—too slow, too exposed—and lifted Scarlett entirely, carrying her and their son in a single, protective embrace.

"You just focus on our son," he whispered. "We're going home."

He carried his family out of the blood-soaked, besieged infirmary and across the tarmac toward the waiting French military helicopter. The rotor wash blasted his face, stinging his eyes with tears he refused to shed. The French Medevac—a direct result of Deedee's sacrifice—was their final, critical escape route, flying them toward a safe, distant military hospital and the promise of a future secured by pure, reckless love.

Chapter 15: The Unseen Wounds

The canteen in the French military hospital was an island of jarring normality. The smell of institutional coffee and stale pastry hung heavy in the air, a world away from the metallic tang of blood and ozone. Arthur sat hunched at a small, Formica table, his body stiff but functional. His friends, Ben and Rhys, sat opposite him, looking equally ravaged but alive.

Rhys reached across the table, sliding a heavy, dented silver flask toward Arthur. "Here, Daddy. Just the cure for a five-hour Medevac hangover."

Arthur nodded his thanks, unscrewing the cap. He poured a generous measure of amber liquid—whiskey—into his weak, lukewarm coffee. Ben did the same. It was a silent ritual, a survival mechanism honed over years of hostile environments.

"She holding up?" Ben asked, quietly, nodding toward the closed steel door that led to the secure patient wing.

"She's sleeping," Arthur replied, taking a long, slow drink. The heat of the whiskey hit his chest, a momentary, welcome burn against the cold fatigue. "Logan's in the incubator—standard procedure, monitoring the chemical load. He screamed strong, though. He's a fighter."

Rhys leaned back, running a hand over the fresh scrape on his scalp. "He had to be, didn't he? Born in a fucking war zone. Look, mate, we've seen some horrible, brutal shit over the last twenty years. We've seen men crack under pressure that wasn't half as bad as that. But Scarlett... she's the toughest operator I've ever seen."

Arthur finally looked up, finding profound relief in the shared observation. "You mean it?"

"I do, mate," Rhys confirmed. "When she told you to shoot the gun while she was pushing? And then used that pain to deliver the head? That's not courage, Arthur. That's *rage*. That woman is a warrior. She didn't have the training, but she had the absolute resolve. She deserves a medal, not a debrief."

Ben nodded, swirling his coffee. "She went from a civilian lawyer to tactical counsel and then delivered a child while half a dozen lunatics were trying to shoot her husband. You're right. We've seen soldiers run;

she stayed put. She didn't just survive; she controlled the whole bloody tempo."

The Fear of the Future

The praise was comforting, easing the sharp edges of Arthur's guilt. But the conversation quickly turned to the future—the domestic battlefield he wasn't trained for.

"I'm terrified, lads," Arthur admitted, the confession raw and quiet, almost startling in its simplicity. "I mean, genuinely. I don't know how to raise a child. I grew up in the system, remember? Foster homes, military barracks. I don't know what a *safe home* looks like unless it's got three fortified layers and a biometric lock."

Rhys snorted, taking a large swig from his mug. "A safe home, you big idiot, is where you are. You're the strongest perimeter on the planet."

"That's the point! My skill set is neutralization, not stability," Arthur countered, leaning his elbows on the table. "I know how to dismantle threats. I don't know how to teach a child to ride a bike without running a full risk assessment on the pavement surface and analyzing pedestrian traffic flow."

Ben sighed, his tone softening with the quiet weariness of a parent. "Look, I know what you mean. The first time I changed little Chloe's nappy, I nearly had a panic attack because the instructions weren't clear enough. It's chaos. It's uncontrolled, relentless, messy chaos. You hate chaos."

"Exactly. I'm hardwired for order," Arthur whispered.

"But you love Scarlett," Ben reminded him gently. "And you love that little squishy thing you were holding."

Rhys laughed, a short, dark sound. "Trust me, Arthur. None of us know what the hell we're doing. I raised two kids while chasing down ex-paramilitary assets in Eastern Europe. My parenting style is best described as 'loud, aggressive supervision.' You will make mistakes. You will lose your temper. But you just keep coming back. You just show up. That's the one thing we actually know how to do. You show up for the fight, and you show up for the family."

"And besides," Ben added, pouring more whiskey into Arthur's coffee. "You've got Scarlett. She's the anchor. She's the one who will make sure he knows the difference between a tactical advantage and sharing his toys. You'll just be the muscle."

The collective wisdom, seasoned with violence and hard-earned love, settled Arthur's nerves. He wasn't alone, and his friends, flawed as they were, were offering the one truth he could rely on.

The Call to Duty

The easy camaraderie broke abruptly. The steel door to the main medical lounge hissed open, and Darren Foote walked in. He looked sharp, clean, and utterly exhausted, carrying a thick satchel that denoted operational business.

He walked straight to the table. "Morning, lads. Congrats, Arthur. Now," Foote said, dropping the satchel onto the Formica with a heavy *thud*, "the doctors said the immediate crisis is over, which means the political one is just beginning. Number 10 is demanding a full debrief on the French deployment, and we have a very active mole digging on our side. We have to make sure our narrative is airtight before they wake Ms. Harper up."

Arthur drained his mug, the warmth of the whiskey and the quiet support of his friends instantly replaced by the cold, necessary weight of command. "Right. Let's talk about Gary's remaining assets. Let's talk about the final pursuit."

Chapter 16: The Wedding Vow

The first sensation Scarlett registered was the quiet. After weeks of roaring seas, grinding machinery, and gunfire, the stillness of the room was profound. It was a cold, clinical quiet, underscored by the gentle, steady hush of the hospital environment. The pain was still a deep, steady throb in her flank, expertly managed by slow-drip narcotics. She felt immense exhaustion, the kind that indicated days, not hours, had passed.

She opened her eyes slowly. The room was bathed in the pale, filtered light of a French military hospital—sterile, white, and fiercely secure. The air was clean. She was safe.

Her gaze swept the room, instantly finding the small plastic bassinet positioned beside her bed. Inside, tiny and bundled in thick white blankets, was Logan. He was still, perfect, and breathing evenly. A profound, consuming wave of relief washed over her, making her breath hitch. Her son was alive.

Her eyes drifted to the chair pulled close to the door. Arthur. He was slumped sideways, head resting against the rough military-grade fabric, his immense frame barely contained by the small chair. He was wearing clean fatigues, but his face was gaunt, unshaven, and streaked with the permanent residue of exhaustion. Even in deep sleep, he remained the sentinel: his strong right hand rested lightly on the pistol tucked securely into the waistband of his trousers.

She watched him sleep, the sheer weight of his vigil evident in the tension of his shoulders. She had survived the hostile environment and the terrifying childbirth, but he had survived the uncertainty.

The New Normal

A nurse entered quietly, checking the monitors, and saw Scarlett awake. The nurse smiled, gave an enthusiastic, hushed confirmation that Logan was doing well and had been given the all-clear, and gently wheeled the bassinet closer. The rhythmic sound of her son's small, immediate breaths was the most beautiful sound Scarlett had ever heard.

The sound of the baby caused Arthur to bolt upright instantly, his hand snapping to the gun. His eyes, dark and bloodshot, were wide with immediate alarm before they focused on her face. The gun hand dropped instantly.

"Scarlett," he breathed, the relief making his voice crack. He was beside her in a second, his weight settling gently on the edge of the bed. "Welcome back, my love."

"You look like a hostage victim," Scarlett whispered, trying to smile, her voice rough.

"I am," he countered, kissing her hand, holding it to his cheek. "But I'm the one who escaped. You—you are the warrior."

They lay in comfortable silence for a long moment, the simple act of breathing in the same room, together, a profound victory.

"You're not leaving again," Scarlett stated, not a question, but a final, absolute declaration.

"Never," Arthur promised. "We start over. We build that life we talked about, the safe one."

"It's going to be chaotic, brilliant, and messy," Scarlett warned him.

"I thrive on messy," he replied, his gaze soft. "By the way, there's a small operational detail you need to know. When we landed in France, I registered us with the French authorities. For security reasons, and to grant me immediate access to your care and Logan's medical decisions, I told them we were legally married. You're officially Mrs. Jacobs now, lawyer."

Scarlett stared at him, a sudden, bright laugh escaping her lips. "You didn't! You absolute, tactical bastard. You hijacked my wedding plans for a code black extraction?"

"I signed the papers," he conceded with a wry grin. "The river stone proposal still stands, but legally, you're already stuck with me."

"Then we need to fix the actual wedding," Scarlett decided, resting her hand on her abdomen. "No more woodsmoke and mud. We need a beach. And a lot of very strong coffee."

The Cost of Survival

Arthur's face darkened, the brief moment of normalcy dissolving. He squeezed her hand, preparing for the inevitable operational pivot.

"We have to talk, Scarlett. Now. The political cleanup is working. Deedee needs an immediate, full debrief on everything that happened in that cell. The lack of immediate medical care, the full details of your father's involvement, the entire layout of the French facility. You were lucid during the worst of it, and your account is the only thing that can solidify the charges against Mr. Harper and ensure we permanently dismantle Gary's network."

Scarlett felt the cold dread return, realizing the fight hadn't ended with the birth. "They want the testimony now?"

"They want it now," Arthur confirmed, his eyes hardening with the necessity of the moment. "Before your father can leverage the legal delay, and before Gary's people contaminate the scene. I know this is asking everything, my love, but we have to finish the war for Logan's future."

Chapter 17: The Counsel's Testimony

The room was cold, quiet, and aggressively functional—a sterile Met briefing room in the secure section of headquarters. It was only 48 hours post-delivery, yet Scarlett was already delivering her testimony. Arthur sat in the back row, his presence a silent guarantee of her safety, but his role was strictly supportive.

He wasn't merely holding his son; he was holding the entire physical reality of the war. Logan, tiny, mottled, and smelling faintly of hospital antiseptic, was tucked safely against Arthur's chest, swaddled tightly in a clean blanket. The low, steady sounds of the infant's breathing were the only domestic noise in the operational space.

Scarlett stood at the head of the long table, illuminated by the harsh fluorescent lights. She was dressed in dark, loose civilian clothes, her face still pale and exhausted, betraying the immense trauma of the high-stress, drugless labor she had endured. But her focus was absolute. She was no longer a civilian asset;

she was Counterintelligence Counsel, the primary witness, and the tactical brain behind the prosecution.

The Unbroken Ledger

"The target was not high-value product, but institutional vulnerability," Scarlett began, her voice clear, though slightly thin from disuse. "The facility in Le Havre was structurally identical to the Manchester compound, indicating a standardized, systemic operational model. The entire French infrastructure was set up and maintained by my father, Mr. Harper, specifically to ensure remote, clean access to a delivery site he controlled."

She moved seamlessly to the whiteboard, using a stylus to display complex network diagrams. Arthur watched, mesmerized and horrified, as she laid bare the extent of Gary's network. She detailed her weeks of forced labor, not dwelling on the physical humiliation, but focusing entirely on the systems she was made to compromise.

"My first move was to create the IP address markers, knowing they would be spotted by a Met analyst,"

Scarlett explained, her voice firm. "But the real work was the counter-intelligence. Gary forced me to lock down his Sterling Coast Property Group files. In doing so, I copied and inverted his entire financial architecture."

She outlined the layers: the shell companies, the false deeds, the manipulation of the Land Registry data. She revealed the specific IP addresses she had covertly implanted in Gary's competitors' systems and the government finance databases—not just to alert the Met, but to create a legally traceable chain of custody.

"Every move I made—every transaction I was forced to process—I left behind a digital fingerprint of his corruption. They thought they were using me to secure their systems; I was using their systems to indict them."

The Price of Clarity

Arthur looked down at Logan, whose small hand was curled around his finger. The child had survived the toxic environment and the brutal entry into the world;

now, he was witnessing the final act of his mother's war.

Arthur was consumed by a dual, violent emotion: immense pride in her intelligence and unrelenting fury over the cost. She was 48 hours post-labor, delivering a perfect, prosecutable case against a global syndicate and her own father, all while recovering from extreme physical trauma.

He thought of the pain in the besieged delivery room, the moment she'd called out his name, and the clinical reality of the birth. He was clear of all charges, his career intact, his family rescued, all because Scarlett had maintained her focus and her will to fight, even when facing death and betrayal.

"The evidence is irrefutable," Deedee confirmed, her voice sober, addressing the gathered brass—a panel of senior detectives and legal counsel. "Ms. Harper not only broke the network's financial core; she handed us the procedural evidence to bypass the institutional protection Mr. Harper provided."

The implication was staggering. They had enough to move on Mr. Harper immediately.

"The charges against Mr. Harper are treasonous," one of the legal counsel noted, his voice hushed. "The use of the MH Yacht and the unauthorized surgical team alone..."

Arthur pulled Logan closer. The external war was over. The charges were secured. But the internal, familial war was about to begin. He knew Mr. Harper's immediate, violent response wouldn't be silence; it would be a desperate, final legal assault to reclaim his social standing and control over his daughter and grandson.

The peace would be temporary. Arthur looked at the monitor displaying the facility blueprint—the place where Logan had been born. He knew they had bought their future, but the payment was still due.

Chapter 18: The Bothy Vow

The cottage air was thick with the scent of woodsmoke, coffee, and powdered milk. Several months had passed since the extraction in Le Havre, and the intensity of the trauma had settled into the exhausting, rhythmic chaos of early parenthood. Scarlett was officially on maternity leave, but her days were a dizzying blend of feeding schedules, sleep deprivation, and high-level legal strategy.

Gary had vanished—a dangerous, silent presence that meant the threat was still active. Meanwhile, her father, Mr. Harper, was relentless. His legal team was wrapping them up in litigation with every move they made against the OCG's finances, attempting to freeze their assets and drag them into civil court for defamation. Scarlett spent her rare moments of quiet not reading baby books, but reviewing case files on her secure laptop.

The cottage had become a strange hybrid: part idyllic moorland home, part covert operations center. Logan, nestled in his now-repaired cot in the nursery, was the undeniable, beautiful center of their universe.

The Vigil and the Exhaustion

Scarlett was perpetually exhausted, her body still recovering from the brutal birth. She would often wake in the middle of the night, reaching for Arthur, only to find the bed cold and empty beside her.

She would inevitably find him in the nursery, slumped deep in the rocking chair, Logan asleep against his chest. His posture would be relaxed, a profound contrast to the rigid tension he maintained during the day. He was still the sentinel, but his focus had shifted from the windows to the tiny, fragile life in his arms.

Arthur always did his share of the night feeds, moving with a controlled, quiet competence that belied his lethal training. He'd spend hours there, rocking his son, his good arm wrapped protectively around the infant. This vigil was his peace, but it was also a visible manifestation of his fear—a fear that if he let down his guard, even in sleep, the world might steal what he had fought so desperately to gain.

The Wedding and the Future

Despite the ever-present threat and the exhaustion, they were determined to build a future. They had started planning the wedding, a final, public declaration of their commitment that would supersede the tactical paperwork Arthur had filed in France.

The location was chosen with pragmatic necessity: a small, sturdy chapel nestled deep in the limestone valleys of the Peak District. They chose St. Stephen's Church, Hassop—a simple, stone-built chapel that blended perfectly with the rough, protective landscape of the moor.

"No grand cathedral," Scarlett had decided. "No guests who aren't vetted by a team of AFOs. Just us, the mountains, and a clear line of fire, just in case."

Arthur had managed a genuine smile. "I'll wear the trauma plate under the suit, just for you, lawyer. And I'll bring the ring."

The planning felt absurdly normal—arguing over the type of flowers versus the location of the nearest secure comms relay. But the normalcy was crucial. Scarlett knew that every moment spent choosing a reading or ordering a small cake was a moment stolen from Gary's influence.

Her work, meanwhile, continued quietly. Every week, she personally reviewed the litigation coming from her father's firm, methodically squashing his attempts to gain access. Gary's silence was the most terrifying element of all. He was consolidating, waiting, and everyone knew that a final, decisive counter-attack was inevitable.

But for now, there was the scent of coffee, the quiet rhythm of the rocking chair, and the beautiful, overwhelming weight of a life secured.

Chapter 19: The Aethelred File Retrieval

The scent of gun oil and brewing coffee clung to Arthur's tactical gear, an appropriate blend of deadly intent and focused professionalism. He stood in the secure briefing room, laying out the schematic maps of the London financial district building—the current location of the asset. He hadn't seen Scarlett or Logan since leaving the cottage 12 hours ago; they were safe, secured by Deedee's local rotation team, but the silence of the comms line was a constant pressure.

"The civil suit from Mr. Harper is running, and the criminal investigation is stalled," Arthur stated, his voice tight. "We need the physical ledger."

His focus was the original Aethelred Group Ledger. The genius of Scarlett's counterintelligence had been the digital flip, but for institutional credibility against a powerful figure like Mr. Harper, the physical documents—the hard copies confirming the initial OCG contract—were necessary. Without them, Mr. Harper could simply claim the Met's digital evidence was fabricated by a disgraced ex-operative and a compromised asset. The Ledger was needed to secure the criminal prosecution against Gary and Mr. Harper.

"Rhys, Ben. Time to earn your triple hazard pay," Arthur dictated, tracing the building's infrastructure. "The file is in London. Mr. Harper archived the original Aethelred dossier in a secure storage facility adjacent to his old firm. We move by train under cover, then switch to a low-profile vehicle Deedee has secured for us near the M1 exit. We get the ledger, and we are gone."

Breaching Protocol: The Financial Heart

The mission was high-risk, a *silent* operation within the financial heart of the city, requiring near-zero compromise.

"We move in civilian clothes, look like late-shift IT maintenance," Arthur instructed. "Rhys, Ben, you'll carry the kit—thermal scanner, cutting torch (battery-powered, minimal signature), and a specialized fiber optic scope. Rhys, you secure the stairwell. Ben, you handle the comms relay and entry into the vault."

Ben, the pragmatic technician, looked at the blueprint. "The archive level is below ground, Arthur. Reinforced concrete vault, single pressure plate door. Standard issue for high-value client assets."

Rhys, the team's security expert, frowned. "We're using the ancient bypass tool, right? The one that won't show up on a standard Met inventory?"

"We're using the ancient bypass tool," Arthur confirmed. "It's the only asset that won't show up on a standard Met inventory."

The logistics were meticulous. They planned the route to avoid every known CCTV and ANPR camera from the M1 into the financial square. They had a 40-minute operational window—the time it would take for the building's internal night security to realize their presence was unauthorized.

"If we encounter resistance, the mission is priority one," Arthur stressed, looking pointedly at Rhys. "Lethal force is a last resort. We are retrieving evidence, not starting a firefight."

Rhys nodded. "Understood. The consequences of a firefight in a London financial building would instantly nullify the political protection Deedee secured."

The Silent Pilgrimage

They moved by night, the train ride into London tense and silent. Arthur, Rhys, and Ben, looking like tired city workers, scanned every face, every exit, every shadow. Once in the city, they picked up a clean, nondescript hatchback.

The drive to the financial square was a silent, grim pilgrimage. They drove to the target building, a towering monument to commerce and secrecy. Arthur paused, pulling his team into the shadow of a recessed loading bay.

"Rhys, you cover the perimeter and comms relay. Ben, you're on the vault door and the thermal scan. I go in first."

Arthur moved toward the service entrance. He had to breach the fortified office, retrieve the ledger, and escape the institutional core of their enemy. The tension was immense, but the retrieval was on.

He looked down at his watch, counting the seconds until the mission clock started. He thought of Logan sleeping peacefully miles away. *I get the file, lawyer. I get the evidence we need to finish this.*

Chapter 20: The Filing and the Fury

The cold, heavy folder containing the original Aethelred Group Ledger lay secured on the table in the cottage kitchen—physical proof of the criminal conspiracy that extended from the dockyards to the city's financial heart. Arthur had returned exhausted but triumphant, the London mission executed with brutal efficiency.

But the silence was short-lived.

A certified courier had delivered a heavy manila envelope to Deedee's secure Met office, which was immediately rushed to the cottage via armed escort. It wasn't a tactical threat; it was a devastating legal assault. The documents were official: Mr. Harper had filed for a Child Arrangements Order (CAO), seeking immediate access and challenging Arthur and Scarlett's fitness to parent, citing their criminal fugitive status and Arthur's "documented history of institutional misconduct."

Arthur read the document, his body going rigid with a fury that felt colder and more dangerous than any he'd shown in combat.

"He's leveraging my military file," Arthur grated, his eyes scanning the detailed citations of his operational errors and recent suspension. "He's using the Met's own dirt against us. This is why he kept the original Aethelred files secure—he knew we'd need them, and he was already preparing his counter-attack."

Scarlett, balancing Logan on her hip while reading the complex affidavits, felt the cold shock give way to professional clarity. The pain of her father's betrayal was absolute, but she recognized the genius of the legal strategy.

The Custody Battle Begins
"This is not a civil suit, Arthur," Scarlett stated, walking toward the secure laptop. "This is a targeted legal demolition. He is leveraging every ambiguity of our past six months—the French marriage, the gunshot wound, the fugitive flight—to prove instability and gain control over Logan."

Arthur slammed his fist onto the table. "I'll find him. I'll drive to his office and end this right now."

"No!" Scarlett snapped, the sound sharp. "You will not engage him physically. That is exactly what he wants—a public outburst to prove his claim of your instability. You are a detective, Arthur. This is my domain."

She sat down at the keyboard, pushing the emotional trauma aside. "Our defense strategy changes now. The Ledger is for the criminal prosecution of Gary and his network. This lawsuit is for our family survival."

"We treat this as an operational command structure, Arthur," she continued, her voice gaining the clipped, authoritative tone he used in the field. "You are my field asset and security detail. I am Lead Counsel. Your job is to secure my environment. My job is to destroy his legal position."

Defense Strategy: Tainting the Source
Scarlett began dictating her demands, her fingers flying across the keys as she organized the digital defense.

"First, we file a motion to dismiss based on Tainted Evidence. He is leveraging documents and information gained through his involvement in organized crime—he used the OCG's power to serve these papers. We turn his legal defense into a liability."

"Second, we counter-file for Full Custody, supervised access only for him. We use the official Met report on his role in the French operation and the fact he threatened to authorize a C-section to kill me and take the child. We use his own treason against him."

Arthur leaned against the doorframe, watching her work—the fury in his eyes slowly transforming into focused purpose. He watched the lawyer he loved, tired and with a baby bundled on her chest, prepare to wage the most dangerous courtroom battle of her life.

"And the wedding?" Arthur asked, the word quiet.

"The wedding," Scarlett confirmed, looking up. "The wedding is our final act of defiance. We are not married ambiguously in France anymore. We are Mrs. and Mr. Jacobs, full stop. We are a family unit. It shuts down his final line of attack. We set the date now."

Arthur smiled, a cold, predatory look returning to his eyes. "Understood, Counsel. Operation Legal Siege is live. Tell me where you need me to stand guard."

Chapter 20: The Filing and the Fury

The cold, heavy folder containing the original Aethelred Group Ledger lay secured on the table in the cottage kitchen—physical proof of the criminal conspiracy that extended from the dockyards to the city's financial heart. Arthur had returned exhausted but triumphant, the London mission executed with brutal efficiency.

But the silence was short-lived.

A certified courier had delivered a heavy manila envelope to Deedee's secure Met office, which was immediately rushed to the cottage via armed escort. It wasn't a tactical threat; it was a devastating legal assault. The documents were official: Mr. Harper had filed for a Child Arrangements Order (CAO), seeking immediate access and challenging Arthur and Scarlett's fitness to parent, citing their criminal fugitive status and Arthur's "documented history of institutional misconduct."

Arthur read the document, his body going rigid with a fury that felt colder and more dangerous than any he'd shown in combat.

"He's leveraging my military file," Arthur grated, his eyes scanning the detailed citations of his operational errors and recent suspension. "He's using the Met's own dirt against us. This is why he kept the original Aethelred files secure—he knew we'd need them, and he was already preparing his counter-attack."

Scarlett, balancing Logan on her hip while reading the complex affidavits, felt the cold shock give way to professional clarity. The pain of her father's betrayal was absolute, but she recognized the genius of the legal strategy.

The Custody Battle Begins

"This is not a civil suit, Arthur," Scarlett stated, walking toward the secure laptop. "This is a targeted legal demolition. He is leveraging every ambiguity of our past six months—the French marriage, the gunshot wound, the fugitive flight—to prove instability and gain control over Logan."

Arthur slammed his fist onto the table. "I'll find him. I'll drive to his office and end this right now."

"No!" Scarlett snapped, the sound sharp. "You will not engage him physically. That is exactly what he wants—a public outburst to prove his claim of your instability. You are a detective, Arthur. This is my domain."

She sat down at the keyboard, pushing the emotional trauma aside. "Our defense strategy changes now. The Ledger is for the criminal prosecution of Gary and his network. This lawsuit is for our family survival."

"We treat this as an operational command structure, Arthur," she continued, her voice gaining the clipped, authoritative tone he used in the field. "You are my field asset and security detail. I am Lead Counsel. Your job is to secure my environment. My job is to destroy his legal position."

Defense Strategy: Tainting the Source

Scarlett began dictating her demands, her fingers flying across the keys as she organized the digital defense.

"First, we file a motion to dismiss based on Tainted Evidence. He is leveraging documents and information gained through his involvement in organized crime—he used the OCG's power to serve these papers. We turn his legal defense into a liability."

"Second, we counter-file for Full Custody, supervised access only for him. We use the official Met report on his role in the French operation and the fact he threatened to authorize a C-section to kill me and take the child. We use his own treason against him."

Arthur leaned against the doorframe, watching her work—the fury in his eyes slowly transforming into focused purpose. He watched the lawyer he loved, tired and with a baby bundled on her chest, prepare to wage the most dangerous courtroom battle of her life.

"And the wedding?" Arthur asked, the word quiet.

"The wedding," Scarlett confirmed, looking up. "The wedding is our final act of defiance. We are not married ambiguously in France anymore. We are Mrs. and Mr. Jacobs, full stop. We are a family unit. It shuts down his final line of attack. We set the date now."

Arthur smiled, a cold, predatory look returning to his eyes. "Understood, Counsel. Operation Legal Siege is live. Tell me where you need me to stand guard."

Chapter 21: The Unseen Thirst

For the first time in months, Logan had gone down for the night without a fight. The sudden domestic quiet was a profound luxury. Scarlett had actually managed to get into the shower and complete her full routine before Arthur returned from his check-in at the Met office in London. She had relished the hour alone, pampering herself in a small attempt to reconnect with the woman who existed before the constant threat.

Stepping out of the shower, she wrapped a dark, soft towel around her body. She glanced at the baby monitor—Logan was still sleeping soundly, his small breathing amplified by the secure unit. She walked toward the dresser, starting the methodical process of rubbing rich moisturizer onto her legs and arms. Pregnancy had undeniably sucked the goodness out of her skin, and her thirties had finally caught up with her, leaving behind lines and textures that felt foreign.

Catching sight of herself in the full-length mirror across the bedroom, she paused. She walked toward it slowly, the moisture cooling on her skin. Standing side-on, she studied her figure's reflection, largely covered by the towel.

She dropped the towel. The sudden, cold exposure was both shocking and necessary. *Christ,* she thought, surveying her body in the harsh light, *were they always that low?* Her hands went to her stomach, tracing the faint, silvery stretch marks from carrying Logan. Despite being back to her former size ten, clothes hung on her differently now. She had a slight softness around the midsection that she despised, and her chest was fuller, heavier.

She couldn't help but wonder if this physical change was the reason she and Arthur hadn't been intimate since before Logan was born. She understood his reluctance towards the end of her pregnancy—she had been the size of a house, and their life had been too dangerous—but now? Was it her new body? They were nearing Logan's first birthday, and absolutely nothing had happened besides their nightly kiss and cuddle before rolling away from each other, facing opposite directions. A cold pang of sadness swept through her. Realistically, they had only been together just over a year, most of it spent fighting for their lives. Maybe he'd simply had enough of her.

That's when she noticed him in the doorway.

The Breakthrough

Arthur stood motionless, his jacket still on, framed by the dim hallway light. The look on his face was one she hadn't seen in a long time, a raw, powerful desire that had been suppressed beneath months of professional fear and exhaustion.

Before she could cover up with embarrassment, his jacket dropped to the floor and his lips were on hers, instantly bridging the gap of months of silence and uncertainty. His hands swept across her body, touching her with a reverence and urgency that answered all her fears.

With one swift movement, he lifted her up, her body pressed against his uniform. Moving backward, he backed her onto the bed, lowering her down without breaking the consuming kiss. His hands moved quickly, seeking the intimacy they had both been denied, and she gasped at the sudden, sharp shock of contact.

He stopped instantly, pulling back, his eyes locked on hers, the soldier demanding consent even in the heat of the moment. "Is this ok, do you want me to stop? I'm not hurting you, am I?"

"Fuck no," she breathed, her hands moving to take his shirt off.

He yanked it off over his head, the suppressed power of his body suddenly unleashed, while her hands clumsily worked at his belt, revealing the hard edge of his hunger. He didn't wait for his trousers to come off before he was driving them together.

Thrusting slowly at first, he waited for her, watching her face. She grabbed his hips and pulled him hard into her, leaning into his rhythm, and that was it. Arthur couldn't control himself any longer. He had been waiting for this for months—waiting for the right moment, for her to be recovered, for the peace to be guaranteed.

Not wanting it to be over too soon, he slowed down again, hitching her legs up onto his hips, rising slightly onto his knees. He devoured the sight of her: his warrior woman. Pregnancy had somehow made her more sensual, her curves more defined, her strength more palpable. He saw the faint pale stretch marks against the scar on her flank, a visible map of their shared trauma and survival.

She reached her climax, her internal tightening enough to shatter his remaining control. They fell onto each other, panting and sweating, the heavy weight of his body pressing her into the mattress, the physical release a profound and necessary anchor to their hard-won reality.

Chapter 22: The Final Legal Siege

The scent of woodsmoke and a lingering, intimate warmth replaced the sterile smells of fear and antiseptic that had dominated their lives for months. Arthur woke before the alarm, a deep, restorative sleep finally granted after the emotional breakthrough of the previous night. He watched Scarlett sleep—she had managed maybe four uninterrupted hours—the marks of strain visibly lessened.

He rose quietly, moving with the practiced, low-impact grace of a soldier who never wants to wake the enemy. His first mission was domestic: Logan.

He moved through the cottage. Logan, nearly one, was already awake, standing in his cot, demanding attention. Arthur checked the comms system, then retrieved Logan, moving straight to the kitchen to start the breakfast routine. He was making coffee and pureeing fruit when the secure line to Deedee rang—the urgent, double-tap encryption signal that meant immediate operational action.

The Injunction Arrives

Arthur answered, his voice tight. Deedee sounded grim, professional, and furious.

"He's moved, Arthur. Mr. Harper filed the motion late last night. It's a full injunction to block the marriage, citing gross institutional negligence by the Met in clearing an unfit former operative. He's leveraging the entire initial fugitive narrative to challenge the validity of the French marriage and demand custody of Logan."

Arthur sat Logan in his high chair, the documents from Deedee printed instantly on the secure terminal. The papers were massive—a complex legal maneuver that targeted every weakness in their official story. Mr. Harper was using the courts as his own private weapon. Arthur felt the familiar cold rage ignite. This wasn't about law; it was about control and destruction.

Arthur slammed his hand onto the table, the impact swallowed by the heavy wood. "He's leveraging my military file," Arthur grated, his eyes scanning the detailed citations of his operational errors and recent suspension. "He's using the Met's own dirt against us.

This is why he kept the original Aethelred files secure—he was preparing his final counter-attack."

The Wedding as a Weapon

Scarlett, drawn by the sound of Arthur's voice, appeared in the doorway, wrapped in a thick dressing gown. She immediately spotted the official documents.

"It's here, isn't it?" she asked, already walking toward the secure tablet.

"The lawsuit. It's the same day as the wedding. He's challenging everything."

Scarlett immediately shifted into "Lead Counsel" mode, pushing aside the mother's anxiety. "The wedding is no longer a personal vow; it's a combat operation. We have to proceed with the ceremony, legally, to nullify his motion, but the entire event is now severely high-risk."

Arthur nodded. The wedding was their final, most crucial piece of the strategic puzzle.

Arthur immediately contacted Rhys and Ben, pulling them from their administrative cover. "New brief, lads," Arthur dictated over the secure channel. "The wedding is a full Code Black event. Mr. Harper has filed a motion to compel, and he's using the church as the battleground. We need to assume hostile physical interception is guaranteed."

Final Security Protocol

Arthur and his team spent the next twelve hours converting a pastoral ceremony into a fortress plan.

Target Analysis: St. Stephen's Church, Hassop, was already selected for its isolation and defensibility.

Arthur reviewed the security plan for the church point by point, holding Logan on his hip while dictating orders:

- Perimeter Lockdown: "Rhys, you run external perimeter command. Thermal surveillance on all approach routes two hours pre-ceremony. Anyone not on the vetted guest list is detained and verified immediately."

- Internal Defense: "Ben, you lead internal security. You and two other AFOs are placed discreetly inside the chapel, acting as civilian guests. You watch the aisle, the windows, and the altar. The moment the warrant is presented, you shield the bride."
- The Escape Route: "We need a designated escape vehicle, engine running, secured within 100 meters of the chapel. If the marriage is completed, and Mr. Harper attempts physical seizure, we exit instantly."

Arthur knew the emotional cost would be immense. Scarlett would be walking down the aisle to a courtroom battle disguised as a marriage vow.

Scarlett placed her hand on Arthur's arm, her eyes though fearful, hardened with immediate resolve. "Then we give him his battle, Arthur. We secure the marriage, and we destroy his claim."

Arthur smiled, a cold, predatory look returning to his eyes. He knew he had secured the love, and now he had secured the most formidable legal weapon he could ask for.

"Understood, Counsel. Operation Legal Siege is live. Tell me where you need me to stand guard."

Chapter 23: The Last Appeal

The silence in the cottage, moments after Arthur left for the Manchester office, was thick with the residue of Operation Legal Siege. Scarlett sat hunched over the kitchen table, the official court documents—Mr. Harper's motion for injunction and custody—spread before her. She was Lead Counsel now, and she was studying the enemy's final position. The legal phrasing was ruthless, leveraging every trauma they had endured to prove instability.

Her legal mind, honed by years of training, understood the cold strategy. But the daughter in her recoiled from the absolute, calculated cruelty. This wasn't merely a legal opponent; this was the man who had raised her. This was the man who was now threatening to use the birth of his own grandson as a weapon.

A profound realization settled over Scarlett: the legal counter-assault she was planning—the Tainted Evidence motion, the defense of their marriage—was necessary, but it wouldn't stop the pain. Only a direct, human appeal could possibly break through her father's institutional armor. It was the highest emotional risk she could take, a move Arthur would immediately veto.

Breaching Protocol

Scarlett retrieved the secure burner phone from its lockbox. Arthur had specifically designated it for official Met communications only, logging every outgoing number. Using it for a personal, non-operational contact with a hostile subject was a flagrant violation of protocol, a betrayal of Arthur's trust she filed away for later guilt.

She sat at the table, her hands trembling not from cold, but from the fear of her father's response. She composed the number—a private, untraceable line she knew her father maintained for his most sensitive business dealings.

He will answer with a legal aide. He will assume this is a defense strategy. He will not be Dad.

The phone rang four times before a smooth, automated voice answered. "You have reached the private line of Mr. Maxwell Harper. State your name and purpose."

"It's Scarlett," she said, forcing the name out, swallowing her fear. "The purpose is family."

A long, agonizing pause followed, the sound of static amplified in the quiet room. Then, Mr. Harper's voice, cold, measured, and immediately professional, cut through the machine. "Scarlett. This line is secured. You understand any contact is now being used as evidence in the civil suit. Who authorized this call?"

"No one authorized it," she replied, gripping the phone. "I'm calling you as your daughter. I know why you're doing this—the money, the reputation, the need to control the narrative. But Dad, this is Logan. Your grandson. He's alive. He's perfect. He needs a family that is safe and whole."

The Unbreakable Armor

Scarlett poured every ounce of human emotion she had left into the appeal. She spoke of the sacrifices her mother made, the distance of her lonely childhood, the pride he once claimed to feel in her legal mind, and the impossible reality of the high-stakes life she was now leading. She told him the charges against him—treason, criminal conspiracy—were irrefutable, and that Gary was not a business partner but a time bomb. She reminded him that every action he took was deepening the legal hole he was digging for himself.

"You can walk away, Dad," she pleaded, her voice thick with unshed tears. "You can step away from the motion. We can give you supervised access to Logan, legally. We can protect your name from the worst of the fallout. But you have to choose your blood over your ledger. You have to choose your daughter."

Mr. Harper listened in silence until she was finished, the total absence of interruption more chilling than rage. When he finally spoke, his voice was flat, devoid of warmth or recognition. "The Aethelred Group is leveraged against three global trusts, Scarlett. Your emotional plea is a clear attempt to bypass established judicial boundaries, showing the court your fundamental instability."

"Dad! Did you hear me? I offered you a way out!"

"The only way out is compliance," he stated, his voice hardening into a final, professional ultimatum. "You will cancel the wedding. You will reject Detective Jacobs. You will return to London, where I can secure you adequate counsel and custody rights for the child. Otherwise, the injunction stands. You made your choice the day you ran with a murderer. I will see you in court, Counselor."

The line clicked dead.

Scarlett slowly lowered the phone. The air in the kitchen felt heavy and cold. The appeal had failed completely, confirming the man she had desperately hoped to reach was utterly consumed by the patriarch and the corporation.

She looked at the clock, noting the exact time of the breach. The phone was wiped clean. She had violated protocol, exhausted her last personal option, and confirmed the enemy's absolute commitment.

You want a war, Dad? Scarlett thought, retrieving the lawsuit papers. *Fine. Let's make it the most expensive legal siege this country has ever seen.* Her resolve was absolute. She was done talking. The fight was back on her terms: as Lead Counsel.

Chapter 24: For Whom the Bell Tolls

The rain was a cold, driving sheet against the rough stone of the cottage when Arthur arrived back from the secure Met office. He killed the engine of the Met-issued vehicle a quarter-mile down the lane, relying on the quiet of the moor to conceal his approach. Before he even reached the threshold, the sound hit him: loud, aggressive, and unmistakable. It was Metallica.

He didn't need to step inside to know the track. The low, ominous bass line and the relentless double-kick drumming were the opening to "For Whom the Bell Tolls." Arthur felt his blood run cold. It wasn't the usual angsty rock they listened to for background noise; this was Scarlett's emotional Code Red—a signal that her calm had fractured and the battle had gone internal.

He expected to find her hunched over the secure terminal, silent and seething, or maybe hiding her tears in the rocking chair.

Instead, he found chaos and contradiction. He walked into the living room, stripping off his heavy covert coat.

Scarlett was positioned squarely in the middle of the room, bouncing Logan vigorously in her arms, her whole body swaying to the relentless, aggressive rhythm of the song. Logan was squealing with laughter, the sheer, immediate joy of the child the only sound louder than the music. Scarlett's eyes, however, were red-rimmed and swollen, confirming his initial fear. She had been crying for hours, but had deliberately forced the external mood into manic joy for Logan's benefit.

"Turn that bloody noise down," Arthur grated, his voice tight.

Scarlett ignored the command, continuing to bounce Logan until the song reached its peak. She settled the now giggling child into his cot. "Welcome home, detective," she said, her voice laced with a brittle sarcasm that meant business. She gave him the full debrief on the failed mission—the emotional appeal, the violation of the secure line, and Mr. Harper's cold, clinical dismissal of her as merely "an attempt to bypass established judicial boundaries."

The Silent Siege

The rest of the evening was a masterclass in silent fury. They moved around the kitchen preparing Logan's food, exchanging snide, whispered commentary beneath the guise of discussing the custody filing.

"You should have known better than to break protocol for an emotional appeal," Arthur murmured, his voice low, his anger rooted in the knowledge that she had exposed herself to a calculated psychological attack. "You gave him free evidence of your instability."

"And you trusted Deedee's comms enough for me to use the secure line at all," Scarlett countered, her voice dangerously soft. "Your tactical risk is institutional; mine was personal. At least I confirmed the depth of the enemy's contempt."

They ate dinner in absolute silence, the tension so thick it felt physical. As soon as Logan was secured in his cot for the night, the dam broke.

"You risked everything we fought for, for a sob story!" Arthur yelled, shoving the armchair aside, his voice cracking with the pent-up stress of the entire Legal Siege operation.

"I risked everything to confirm my father is the monster I suspected!" Scarlett shouted back, tears of exhaustion and anger finally streaming down her face. "You want me to be a machine, Arthur! I am fighting for a future that has no security, no money, and no name! I needed to know if I had a father or just a powerful enemy! You can shoot a gun; I have to deal with the fucking consequences!"

The Final Fracture and Return

The fight was brutal, fueled by their mutual guilt and fear. It was the first time they had truly yelled, their perfect control finally shattering under the pressure of the custody battle.

The fight ended not with a resolution, but with a sudden, devastating tactical move by Scarlett. She broke away from Arthur, walking swiftly to the bedroom.

"Where are you going?" Arthur demanded, following her.

Scarlett grabbed her worn walking boots. She purposefully tossed her burner phone—the one carrying the secure comms app—onto the duvet. "I'm going for a walk," she said, her voice shaking but firm. "You can't follow me, Arthur. You have to stay here and protect our son. I need air."

Before he could process the full meaning of her action, she was out the door. Arthur rushed to the window, watching her silhouette disappear into the cold, black expanse of the moor. He grabbed the phone—dead and silent—and realized the chilling truth: she had left the essential operational link behind precisely so he couldn't risk leaving Logan to pursue her. She had forced the separation.

Arthur sat vigil in the rocking chair, Logan whimpering softly against his chest, the fear of what she was doing in the dark consuming him entirely. The hours dragged, the silence of the night occasionally broken by the desperate cry of a distant owl. Three AM came and went.

Then, at 3:15 AM, he heard the front door creak softly. He went rigid, his senses screaming ambush, before he saw the familiar, dark silhouette attempt to slip through the living room.

Arthur reached out and flipped the main light switch.

Scarlett froze, illuminated in the harsh light, soaked by the damp moor air. She was very drunk, her eyes unfocused, swaying unsteadily.

"Don't look at me, you bastard," Scarlett slurred, her voice thick. "I'm not your prisoner." She grabbed the nearest thick wool blanket from the sofa and hurled it at his chest. "Stay the fuck away from me tonight!" she screamed, before storming into the bedroom and slamming the door.

Arthur stood motionless, the blanket draped uselessly over his arm, his body absorbing the verbal violence. He had never seen her that furious, never heard her shout like that. The silence that followed was agonizing.

He waited ten minutes, checking the cottage perimeter before slowly opening the bedroom door. Scarlett was already asleep, passed out face-first on the duvet, lying in nothing but her knickers and a soaked jumper. The large, empty bottle of Jack Daniel's lay on the wooden floor beside the bed.

He carefully covered her with the blanket she had thrown at him, retrieving the empty bottle. He looked at her bruised, exhausted face, wondering if he'd just fucked things up with her beyond repair. He retrieved the empty bottle, turned off the light, and went back to the nursery, choosing the discomfort of the rocking chair and the safety of his son over the cold, empty space in their bed.

Chapter 25: The Hangover Siege

The light filtering through the heavy curtains was not soft morning light; it was a physical weapon. Scarlett squeezed her eyes shut, but the throbbing behind her temples intensified, synchronized perfectly with the relentless ringing in her ears. Every muscle in her body felt loose and useless, a direct, chemical consequence of the Jack Daniel's she had consumed at 3:00 AM. Shame, cold and toxic, was a constant partner to the headache.

She finally dragged herself upright. The kitchen, directly below the bedroom, became a deliberate soundstage for her misery. Arthur was home, and he was absolutely furious.

The Domestic Battlefield

Scarlett knew instantly this wasn't accidental noise. This was calculated, operational warfare designed to exploit her current condition. Arthur, impeccably clean, was sitting on the floor, perfectly dressed, encouraging Logan's most ear-splitting activities.

"Morning, Mrs. Jacobs," Arthur greeted, his voice sharp and utterly devoid of warmth.

Scarlett ignored the sarcasm, moving directly to the kitchen, attempting to brew herself the strongest coffee humanly possible. Arthur followed, maintaining a three-foot perimeter.

"You needed air," Arthur stated, his voice tight with controlled fury. "I get that. What I don't get is why you compromised our entire position for a theatrical exercise."

"I needed to know I had a father, Arthur, or just an enemy," Scarlett retorted, clutching her head. "I had to try one last time. You want to scold me for a violation of the rulebook?"

"I am scolding you for leaving our son vulnerable!" Arthur corrected, his voice rising, slamming a plastic bowl onto the counter. "You chose a childish, selfish walk into the dark, instead of using your brain. That phone was our only link. You left me trapped here, in the dark, helpless—exactly how I felt when they grabbed you on the pavement."

"And you just proved you can't see past the protocol!" Scarlett shot back, the headache forgotten beneath the rush of emotional clarity. "I was begging for connection! I was trying to resolve a twenty-year-old hurt! But you just saw a broken link in your chain of command, Arthur, and you scolded me like a disobedient child. You treat me like an asset that needs to be controlled, not a wife who needs support!"

The Final Showdown

The words hung heavy and absolute. Arthur stared at her, recognizing the devastating truth of her accusation. His fear of losing her *again* had manifested as overbearing, demeaning control.

"I'm sorry about the fight," Scarlett whispered, the anger draining away, replaced by profound regret over the damage they inflicted on each other.

"The consequence of your action isn't going to be an apology," Arthur replied, his voice flat, exhausted. "The consequence is operational. You broke the primary rule: Never give the enemy insight into our psychological status. You confirmed our fragility. I'm going to the office to run a deep-scan to check for digital blowback. When I get back, we will be implementing a new level of security."

Arthur's eyes hardened, delivering the final mandate: "You are not leaving this cottage for six months, Scarlett. You will wear the wire, and we will talk through every emotional response you have."

Scarlett's eyes flashed with absolute, cold rebellion. "The fuck I will! You fucking control freak! The only thing you have any say in is Logan!" she shouted back, stepping directly into his defensive space. "I'll go where the fuck I want when I want. I'm a grown ass fucking woman, you absolute tool!"

Arthur stared back at her, completely disarmed by her explosive response. His professional framework—the one thing he relied on—had been dismantled by one simple truth: he had no authority over her.

"Fuck this! It's my turn to walk!" Arthur responded angrily, grabbing his keys and his jacket. He didn't look back. He shoved the front door open, letting it slam violently against the stone wall.

He rushed out to the car, his movements jerky with pure rage, throwing himself into the driver's seat. As he started the engine, he glanced up at the cottage window.

Scarlett was standing there, framed in the glass, her hand firmly giving him the middle finger.

He drove away, the roar of the engine drowning out the laughter that followed him into the moor. His control was gone. The siege had just begun.

Chapter 26: The Price of the Pint

The roar of the engine was the only thing louder than the rage consuming Arthur. He drove the Met-issued vehicle hard and fast across the moorland roads, not toward his secure office, but toward Manchester—specifically, toward the one man who had successfully navigated the domestic landscape of commitment and chaos: Rhys.

Rhys was Arthur's oldest friend, his loyalty forged over years in environments where trust meant survival. Rhys had married Emily when they were both barely eighteen, just a week before they shipped out on their first exercise. That improbable marriage had somehow endured two decades, four children, and multiple tours with the Special Reconnaissance unit. Rhys's life—a busy, chaotic home anchored by routine—was the precise opposite of Arthur's isolated, operational existence.

Arthur pulled up to Rhys's modest, semi-detached house in the Manchester suburbs. It was 10:00 AM. The house was loud, vibrant, and messy. Rhys met him at the door, spotting the white-knuckle grip on the steering wheel and the simmering fury in Arthur's eyes.

"Jesus, Arthur. Come in," Rhys said, pulling him inside. "The op isn't until Monday. What the hell happened? You look like you just failed a debrief on the wife."

The Unofficial Debrief

Arthur found himself sitting on the edge of Rhys's worn sofa while Logan's contemporaries—Max (10), Leo (7), and Lily (4)—swirled around him, oblivious to the high-level operational stress radiating from the two men. Rhys shooed the kids out.

Rhys returned with a tray holding two mugs of strong tea and his heavy, familiar silver flask. "Start at the top. The truth, mate. Leave the jargon out."

Arthur launched into the rant immediately, the words spilling out, fueled by the guilt of the last 24 hours. He started with the legal filing and ended with the shame of the middle finger seen through the window.

"She called me a child, Arthur. You applied a tactical protocol to a personal crisis. That's your mistake."

"My mistake is loving someone who actively sabotages their own security! She knows the rules! She knows the danger! She's a liable asset!"

Rhys took a long drink. "She's not an asset, mate. She's the mission. And you cannot debrief a wife like she's a suspect who breached comms protocol. She was testing you. She was forcing you to see her pain."

"She made me helpless, Rhys! She left the burner phone behind so I was trapped with Logan! She left me alone, fearing she was dead, when she was drunk in a petrol station miles away!"

Rhys leaned forward. "That fear, Arthur, that helplessness? That's what she felt for nine months, and you dismissed it as 'hormones.' She made you experience the consequence of her feeling unheard. That's what marriage is: forcing the other person to feel what you feel. You're trained to fight enemies; you have to learn how to surrender to your wife."

The Last Drink

The conversation continued for hours, moving from the cottage to the tactical realities of marriage. Arthur drank steadily, seeking the numbness the alcohol provided. Rhys, ever the anchor, paced the house, managing his own chaotic family while maintaining the solemnity of the intervention.

"I can't go back there tonight, Rhys," Arthur mumbled, resting his head against the cool stone wall. "I can't face her. I'm too much of a failure."

"Stay," Rhys conceded. "We'll run the deep-scan from here, and you can sleep on the sofa. But you call her first thing, mate. You don't leave a loose end like that."

Arthur agreed. He slept a heavy, dreamless sleep of exhaustion and chemical oblivion.

The Final Consequence

Arthur woke at 5:30 AM, instantly sobered by the cold realization of his absence. He didn't wait for coffee or a proper goodbye. He grabbed his jacket, thanked Rhys with a curt, mumbled promise, and was out the door.

He drove back to the cottage at lethal speed, rehearsing his apology. He would apologize for the lack of trust, the scolding, the anger, and the drinking. He would surrender control.

He pulled up to the cottage at precisely 6:05 AM. The front door was slightly ajar, disturbed by the wind.

Arthur stopped the car. The immediate, cold dread in his stomach was worse than any gunshot wound. He ran, throwing the door wide.

The cottage was silent.

The kitchen was clean. Logan's high chair was empty. The nursery was empty. The quiet was absolute.

Arthur ran to the bedroom. The bed was stripped. The rocking chair was empty. Scarlett's suitcase, which she always kept under the bed, was gone.

Scarlett had left. She hadn't waited for his apology. She had taken Logan and vanished.

Arthur stumbled back into the living room, his tactical focus dissolving into white-hot panic. He grabbed the secure phone. The phone was dead. He looked at the window, the sun starting to rise over the moor. He was alone with the silence, and the fight had just escalated into a full-scale institutional search.

Chapter 27: The Surveillance of Silence

The cottage was empty, but Arthur was watching. He sat hunched over the main unit terminal in the secure Met office, the cold knot of dread in his stomach tightening with every minute that passed since his return at 6:05 AM to an abandoned house. Rhys and Ben were out, following the logical land routes Scarlett might have taken, but Arthur knew the truth lay in the CCTV logs.

He fast-forwarded the video feed, reviewing the hours of silent surveillance he'd recorded overnight, documenting the events that occurred *after* he left and *before* he returned, leading up to her 2 AM departure.

The Domestic Vigil

The video feed of Saturday evening began:

Scarlett carried on with her domestic routine, her movements deliberate and focused—a woman trying desperately to impose order on external madness. She spent a long time in the kitchen cleaning up the remnants of their disastrous argument and Arthur's snapped control. She moved Logan into the living room, playing quietly with him on the rug.

At precisely 7:00 PM, she settled Logan into his cot for the night. Arthur watched the footage of her emerging from the nursery, her face etched with exhaustion, but the task complete. She then collapsed onto the sofa in the living room, wrapping herself in a blanket and turning on Netflix.

Arthur felt a twist of shame as he watched the footage, seeing the consequence of his absence. *I should have been there. I had twenty minutes to calm her down, and I chose to leave.*

The clock on the surveillance feed ticked onward, charting her quiet, solitary existence. She sat on the sofa, seemingly relaxed, only occasionally checking the time on her wrist, her movements becoming more agitated after midnight.

The Strategic Departure

The pivotal moment occurred at approximately 2:00 AM.

On the video feed, Scarlett suddenly bolted upright on the sofa. She glanced sharply at the clock, her eyes wide with a cold, desperate resolve. She stormed to the bedroom.

The hallway camera captured the frantic, devastating choreography of her exit. The camera was soundless, but Arthur could infer the noise. Scarlett, now visible in the frame, was holding her phone in the crook of her neck, wedged between her ear and shoulder, arguing with someone while simultaneously packing her large suitcase. The camera didn't pick up anything she was saying, but the tension in her jaw and the frantic speed of her hands conveyed the urgency.

Jonesy offered the only auditory confirmation of the escalating crisis. The ginger cat, startled by the noise, padded out onto the landing and settled near the suitcase, the sound of his occasional purr the only sound the camera microphone picked up.

Scarlett finished the packing in a devastating hurry, hauling the massive suitcase onto the landing. The camera picked up the sight of her pausing by the top of the stairs, her shoulders shaking. The footage confirmed she was crying.

She quickly went into Logan's room and packed him a bag too, haphazardly shoving clothes, nappies, and blankets into a soft travel bag. Her focus was not on organization, but on speed.

She then began dragging the bags down the stairs, her haste overwhelming her caution. She slipped violently on the few bottom steps, recovering quickly but letting out a sound the camera captured perfectly: "Fuuuck!"

Getting up immediately, she shoved the bags aside and focused on logistics. She retrieved Logan's sturdy, all-terrain pram and set it up, her movements now efficient and controlled. She walked back upstairs, retrieved Logan, and settled him into the pram.

Scarlett then left the cottage, pushing the pram and dragging the suitcase behind her across the rough stone track. She left on foot, which meant she wouldn't be far, but Arthur knew the capacity of her resolve. She'd be far as a furious woman whose husband had been out all night abandoning her and their child would get—which was further than any of his trained men would expect.

The final frame showed the cottage empty, the front door closed, and the two small bags and pram track marks in the mud leading relentlessly away from their supposed safe house.

I will provide Chapter 28, "Seven Miles of Silence," in full, incorporating all the corrections to the timeline (midday arrival), the clothing (no borrowing), the logical necessity of the walk, and the final, devastating arrival of Arthur on foot.

Chapter 28: Seven Miles of Silence

The initial frantic need to flee the cottage had been fulfilled. Scarlett had walked seven agonizing miles, dragging Logan's heavy pram and her massive suitcase, until she reached the only light visible on the map—*The Old Mill Inn*. She collapsed against the rough stone wall, the sheer, crushing physical effort consuming every ounce of her strength. Her back screamed, her legs felt like lead, and the lingering dread of the last 24 hours was a dull ache in her gut.

She had secured a small, clean room upstairs hours ago, relying on the cover story of the stranded traveler. Now, she was ready to face the world again.

She pulled clean clothes from her suitcase—expensive, soft fabrics, a deliberate choice to reject the filth of the last year. She managed to secure a strong coffee from the pub below, and took Logan out into the small, enclosed pub garden. It was around midday now, and the sun was strong enough to offer a brief, fragile illusion of peace.

The Internal Reckoning

The initial, frantic need to flee Arthur had subsided, replaced by a cold, hard review of her actions. *She didn't know if she was leaving AJ,* but she knew she needed to think. Her walk-out had been fueled by a desperate desire to break Arthur's absolute, suffocating control—the constant surveillance, the tactical judgments, the failure to see her as anything other than an asset.

She knew she had to go home. The child needed stability, routine, and two parents. Her reckless act had given Mr. Harper ammunition, confirming Arthur's darkest accusations about her instability. She couldn't fight a political war against her father from a distance; she needed to be back in the cottage, back on the secure network, and back in her role as Lead Counsel.

She needed solitude to process the trauma of the custody battle and the looming finality of the wedding.

A Moment of Reprieve

Scarlett was interrupted before she could open her secure laptop.

A man approached the wooden picnic table. He was strikingly tall, around 6 feet 7 inches, and possessed a large, powerful muscular build. His olive skin was glistening faintly in the sun, and his expensive athletic wear screamed leisure. *Gym fit,* Scarlett instantly assessed, *not combat fit.* His smile was wide, easy, and completely non-threatening.

"Mind if I join you?" he asked, his voice smooth. "It's the only sunny spot."

He introduced himself as Tyrone. He didn't seem to care about the 11-month-old asleep in the pram next to her, or the river stone engagement ring on her finger, which she had consciously kept visible. He shamelessly, effortlessly flirted. He asked her trivial, meaningless questions about the inn, her fictional

Airbnb troubles, and the challenges of traveling with a baby.

The interaction was a surreal, necessary reprieve. It was a pleasant, mundane distraction from guns, comms, and the threat of institutional betrayal. It was a brief, harmless escape from the suffocating intensity of Arthur's operational love.

Tyrone leaned against the table, casually pulling a cigarette packet from his pocket and lighting one. "Rough night?" he asked, offering her the packet.

She hadn't smoked since university, but the need for a moment of chemical, calming release was immediate. She accepted, inhaling the sharp, calming smoke. The casual intimacy of the moment felt intensely foreign, a brief slip back into a life free of AFO protocols.

"You look like you've been fighting a war," Tyrone noted, his eyes crinkling. "You deserve a break."

"Something like that," Scarlett conceded, inhaling deeply. She felt lighter, the burden of the last year momentarily eased by the attention of a man who saw only a beautiful woman, not a liability.

The Final Arrival

"I think I need to get back inside," Scarlett said finally, stamping out the cigarette. The break was over. She was ready to face the music.

"Ah, shame," Tyrone replied, smoothly taking her hand. "Here's my number. If you're ever lost again, give me a shout."

Scarlett merely smiled, pulling her hand away. "I think I know exactly where I need to be."

She turned, ready to wheel Logan back into the warmth of the inn and call Arthur.

That's when she saw him.

Arthur was standing on the gravel path leading from the main road. He must have been tracing her seven-mile route by foot, driven by sheer, desperate instinct after analyzing the CCTV logs and recognizing the general direction she had taken. His entire posture was rigid, covered in the visible, frantic evidence of his own long, exhaustive search. He took in the entire scene in a split second: Scarlett, leaning against the wall, smelling of fresh smoke, Tyrone—a massive, handsome stranger—standing entirely too close, their pram nearby.

Arthur's face was dark, twisted with a cold, absolute jealousy and fury that surpassed any operational rage he had ever displayed. He hadn't just found her; he had found her in a moment of emotional betrayal, confirmed by the evidence of the cigarette smoke and the handsome man. The fight for control had just resumed, and the real cost of her walk-out was about to be paid.

Chapter 29: The Cost of Air

The final seven miles of the search had been brutal. Arthur's chest still heaved, his muscles screaming from the sheer emotional effort of the frantic drive after analyzing the CCTV logs. Knowing a woman pushing a pram could only cover that distance in one direction, Arthur had simply followed the logical road verge in the Met-issued vehicle he had driven away in.

He stopped dead on the gravel path leading to *The Old Mill Inn*. The rage that had driven him was instantly complicated by a cold, searing pain that was purely personal: jealousy.

The scene was intimate and wrong. Scarlett, his wife and Counterintelligence Counsel, was leaning against the stone wall, the sun catching the faint scar on her flank. She smelled of fresh smoke—a betrayal of their health protocol—and was talking, her head tilted back, to a figure who was everything Arthur was not: massive, relaxed, and utterly non-operational. Tyrone was a physical anomaly, easily six feet seven inches of gym-fit muscle, his olive skin glistening faintly in the midday sun. He held Scarlett's gaze with an easy confidence that Arthur, covered in sweat and paranoia, had forgotten how to project.

Arthur took in the evidence: the proximity, the shared cigarette smoke (meaning a break in her defiant no-smoking rule), the fact that Scarlett had accepted the casual intimacy of a stranger. He didn't see a threat; he saw a consequence. She had gone searching for a release from his control, and she had found it in the arms of a handsome distraction.

The Fight and The Blow

Arthur didn't roar; he moved with the controlled, frightening silence of a predator who has locked onto a target. He walked directly toward the table, ignoring the exhaustion.

Tyrone was the first to react, sensing the shift in the atmosphere. He dropped Scarlett's hand, his smile faltering as he took in Arthur's immense, unreadable frame and the feral exhaustion in his eyes.

"Arthur," Scarlett said, the sound laced with immediate relief and genuine happiness. "You found us! I was just about to call you. I needed to think."

Arthur ignored her, his gaze locked on Tyrone. "The party's over, pal." Arthur's voice was low, flat, carrying the implicit threat of lethal capability.

Tyrone, offended by the summary dismissal, immediately bristled. "Who the hell are you to give orders, mate? If she was my wife, I'd never leave the bedroom. Maybe you should keep a better eye on your property."

Arthur's control snapped. He lunged, but Tyrone shoved him hard in the shoulder. Arthur staggered back, momentarily stunned by the sharp pain of the impact.

Tyrone, fueled by bravado, swung a heavy fist toward Arthur's jaw.

The fight exploded. Scarlett, screaming, tried to wedge herself between them. Tyrone's punch missed Arthur completely and connected, with savage, audible force, with Scarlett's face.

She went down instantly, falling hard onto the gravel. For a terrifying, suspended second, Arthur thought she was out. Tyrone, horrified and momentarily distracted, stared down at her.

Then, fueled by sheer, agonizing pain and residual fury from her abuse in the cells, Scarlett moved. She pushed herself up from the gravel, her eyes cold, pure black rage. She launched herself forward and punched Tyrone squarely in the face.

The sound was a sickening, wet *CRACK*. Tyrone dropped like a bowling pin, his massive body hitting the ground with a soft thud.

Arthur stared at Scarlett—his counsel, his wife—her face bruised, her small frame heaving, but standing over a giant she had just floored with one clean shot. He was impressed, but the immediate crisis was paramount.

The Honest Debrief

Arthur grabbed her arm. "Jesus Christ, Scarlett! That was spectacular. Now, get your bags from the room! I'll get Logan in the car. We need to go now!"

As they settled into the car, leaving the defeated Tyrone to his fate, Arthur's suppressed jealousy flared one last time. "Is that what you want? A gym fit bellend?"

Scarlett snapped out of her exhaustion, her voice suddenly laced with weary honesty. "Oh for fuck sake, Arthur, I bummed a cig off him and he took it as a hint. But hang on a minute, what I want? I'm not the one who left and didn't come back."

Arthur flinched, the accusation hitting its target. "I forgot to ring you."

"Yeah right," she snapped, staring out the window. "You were watching me on your fucking cameras, punishing me by staying out."

Realizing the profound depth of her belief, Arthur pulled the car over immediately. The only sound was Logan playing quietly with a toy in his car seat. He turned to face her. "I went to see Rhys, got drunk, passed out, I came home as soon as I woke up. I didn't look at the cameras once. I just woke up and started driving."

Scarlett looked at the raw honesty in his face. Her anger evaporated, replaced by a sudden, aching understanding. She leaned over and surprised him with a fierce kiss. "You're ridiculous," she sighed, resting her head against his shoulder. "But so am I."

She pulled back, the resolve hardening in her eyes. "We need a break."

Arthur stammered, the old fear of abandonment returning. "What, you want a break? From me?"

"No," she said, squeezing his hand. "We need a break, as in a reset. This whole fight was pathetic and toxic. It's because we're close to snapping."

The crisis was resolved with a shared purpose. They had retrieved their family, and now they needed to reset the clock.

Chapter 30: The New Asset

The small cottage garden, though rugged and overlooked by the imposing moorland, was ablaze with color. Red and blue bunting fluttered against the grey stone walls, and a cheap plastic paddling pool, thankfully dry, was filled with brightly colored balls. Logan was celebrating his first birthday, and Scarlett watched him with a heart full of weary, hard-won joy as he took wobbly, determined steps across the worn patio.

It had been one month of agonizing effort since the incident at the inn. The public fight, the raw admission of toxicity, and Arthur's subsequent decision to prioritize communication had fundamentally changed their relationship. Arthur was still the sentinel—the security protocol was non-negotiable—but he was trying. He used "Counsel" only in briefings, checked his anger before imposing control, and asked before acting. Their trust had stabilized, but the fragility remained.

The party was small and heavily vetted—a gathering of the Jacobs Family Protection Detail disguised as a birthday celebration. The guests included: Arthur,

Scarlett, Logan, Jonesy (who tolerated the guests with feline condescension), Deedee Hayes, and the entire Met-vetted support crew: Rhys, his wife Emily, and their four children: Chloe (14), Max (10), Leo (7), and Lily (4); Ben, his girlfriend Jess (the analyst), and their child, Freddie (2); and Jade, who, despite the betrayal of her own family, was the first to arrive, bringing the cake.

The New Command

As the afternoon wore on and Logan finally collapsed into a cake-induced nap, Deedee approached Scarlett, pulling her away from the noisy cluster of well-wishers toward the relative quiet near the stone wall. Deedee's smile was warm, but her eyes held the sharp, clinical intensity of command.

"First, the good news, Scarlett," Deedee began, her voice low. "The nursery situation is solved. Logan has a secured spot at the Met's crèche starting the moment your maternity leave ends. It's vetted, discreet, and subsidized. You go back to work, he goes to the safest place we can put him."

Relief, pure and immense, washed over Scarlett. "Deedee, thank you. That eliminates 90% of the risk."

Deedee nodded, then her tone shifted, becoming grave. "Now, the real reason I came up here."

"The criminal inquiry into Mr. Harper is entering its final stage. We need clean access, in the field, where our compromised assets can't be recognized. And that's where you come in."

Scarlett frowned, anticipating a desk job. "I'm ready for the Legal Analyst position. I want to build the case against my father."

"That job is secure," Deedee agreed. "But the orders from the Director's office are clear: Headquarters wants to invest in you as a primary asset."

Deedee leaned closer, her eyes glittering with ambition and strategy. "Scarlett, you're unique. You have a barrister's mind for detail, a hacker's ability to penetrate complex systems, and you're female. A clean slate. An absolute weapon. We need you to train as a full operative."

Scarlett's mind reeled. "You mean... weapons? Combat? Undercover?"

"Everything," Deedee confirmed. "Guns, hand-to-hand, deep-cover insertion. If we can plant you in an OCG operation in the future—as the lawyer, the accountant, the civilian—you can bypass every security layer designed to stop Arthur or Ben. You would be more effective than any agent currently on file."

The Burden of Secrecy

The idea was terrifying, exhilarating, and deeply logical. It answered the constant yearning she felt to do more than simply process the aftermath. But the next words Deedee spoke caused a cold, sharp spike of absolute dread.

"Arthur can't know, not yet," Deedee stated firmly. "He will veto this immediately. His protective mandate is absolute, and he will claim this violates your ongoing recovery and his job security. He has veto power over any high-risk assignment involving you. The operational benefit of your skillset is too high to risk his interference."

Scarlett's stomach dropped. *She had just resolved the most toxic fight of their marriage by demanding honesty, and now her boss was demanding she construct the largest lie.*

"We'll frame the training as mandatory specialized legal briefings in London. We're talking three hours a day, five days a week, for three months. I'll handle the official communication with him, citing operational confidentiality and the new role requirements. Your job is to make sure he believes the cover story."

Scarlett felt an immense wave of guilt, heavy and sickening. She looked at Arthur across the lawn, who was stacking empty cake plates, his body relaxed and open in a way she hadn't seen for months. They had fought so hard to dismantle the armor; now she was being forced to rebuild a wall of lies, layer by layer, against the man who was her shield.

"Understood," Scarlett whispered, her jaw set. "The training starts when my leave ends. But Dee, you handle the cover story. I need you to brief Arthur on the travel and the security risks. I can't look him in the eye and lie about this."

Deedee nodded, her expression grim. "I'll initiate the comms sequence after the party. Now, go cut the cake, Counsel. We need to look normal."

Scarlett looked back toward the garden, where Arthur was laughing with Logan, his face a picture of hard-won domestic peace. She felt the surge of pride—she was capable of this lethal transformation—and the cold, hard weight of the impending deception. She was keeping the most critical secret of their marriage hidden, and the fight for their future had never been more dangerous.

Here is the full Chapter 31, "The Live Feed," incorporating the logistical correction for the helicopter transport and the sustained emotional tension of the scene.

Chapter 31: The Live Feed

The small, constant hum of the secure Met office had become Arthur's routine. It was late Tuesday evening. Arthur was reviewing a complex set of offshore trust documents when the alarm klaxon—the high-pitched, insistent tone reserved for breaches of national security—sounded through the office.

He was instantly on his feet, sidearm drawn.

"Arthur! War Room! Now!" Rhys roared, skidding to a halt outside the door. "This is Code Red. Not Gary. Worse."

Arthur followed, his adrenaline spiking. The War Room was a beehive of frantic, low-voiced activity. Deedee stood before the main screen, looking drawn and lethal.

"Status, Deedee," Arthur demanded, moving past the analysts.

"Jacobs. Thank God," Deedee breathed. "We have a critical asset pinned down in a secure data facility near Birmingham. Target: Russian OCG hub. Asset: Female, low profile, identified as *Counsel*." The information was clinical, anonymous, and terrifyingly familiar.

Then, the tactical team flipped the main video feed to the asset's live body camera footage.

The camera was bouncing wildly, the visuals alternating between dark, smoky concrete walls and muzzle flashes. A woman, moving low and fast through a stairwell, was firing a compact weapon, her breathing harsh and amplified by the mic.

Arthur froze. His blood turned to ice, and the floor seemed to tilt violently beneath him. He was scanning the visual for the distinguishing mark—the movement, the hair, the suit—but the camera was too chaotic.

Then, the operative vaulted over a broken console near what looked like a derelict reception desk. For a split second, the body cam caught a clear, undeniable reflection in the shattered floor-to-ceiling mirror fixed to the wall.

It was Scarlett.

Tactical Takeover

"Deedee," Arthur stated, his voice a low, terrifying rasp that silenced the entire room. "Why the *hell* is my wife operating in a hot zone?"

Deedee didn't flinch. "*The Director ordered specialized combat training. We knew you would veto it. She's been a full-spectrum operative for three months, Arthur.*"

Arthur processed the betrayal and the strategic necessity instantly, the soldier taking command.

"Ben, Rhys! Gear up! We're rolling now! Foote, get the Medevac pre-approved for Birmingham! We need a clean extraction route five minutes ago!"

He shoved the console aside, taking command of the tactical screen. "Asset is moving too slow! That weapon—it's the Met-issued P30. She only has one magazine left. The hostiles are suppressing fire, they're not committing. They know they have the advantage."

He recognized her struggle immediately. The target was supposed to be empty. Now she was pinned down by professional security who were fighting aggressively to protect the server farm.

"She's hacking the internal comms now—she's trying to blind them!" Arthur observed, noting a sudden static spike on the audio feed. "Rhys, Ben! Deploy on the south roof access! She's moving toward the central server hub! She needs immediate air support!"

Arthur grabbed the direct comms link to the asset—the comms link he didn't even know she possessed until two minutes ago.

"Scarlett! This is Arthur! You hear me? What is the objective?"

Her voice, tight, strained, but filled with immense defiance, cut through the static. "*Arthur? You hear me? Status is hostile, three down. My objective is the server. I need ten seconds on the hub. Don't worry about the shooting. Just cover the perimeter!"*

"Ten seconds! That's all you get!" Arthur roared.

He watched her sprint across an open section of the floor and dive behind a server rack. The audio feed confirmed the rapid, furious tapping of a keyboard. *She's still trying to complete the file transfer.*

Success was immediate. A notification flashed across the screen: ACCESS GRANTED. DATA TRANSFER INITIATED.

But the hostiles knew she had won. A final, sustained burst of automatic weapon fire slammed into her cover. The camera feed instantly tumbled sideways, showing only concrete and flashing lights. Scarlett's audio feed was replaced by a sharp, agonizing gasp, followed by a heavy, sickening sound of impact.

Arthur stood rigid, his world collapsing for the second time. The immediate order snapped from his mouth: "Foote! Divert the Medevac to our position now! We are taking the air route to Birmingham! We need immediate launch!" The extraction had just become a race against time, and against death.

Chapter 32: The Asset Triumphant

The sound of the final burst of automatic weapon fire slammed into the server rack, immediately followed by the searing, blinding heat in Scarlett's left arm. Her scream was swallowed by the chaos. She didn't drop the terminal; she collapsed onto the floor, the keyboard still under her fingertips, her entire world reduced to the blinding agony radiating from her upper arm.

No, she thought, the word a desperate, internal command. *Not now.*

She forced herself to roll, using the adrenaline to ignore the shock. She pulled the sleeve of her tactical jacket down, then up, tearing the fabric with her teeth. The wound was high on her left arm, a neat, small entry point and a corresponding exit point—a clean "through and through" shot, missing the bone and the major arteries, but bleeding profusely and already setting her limb on fire. It was excruciating, but manageable. Lethal, only if she panicked and bled out.

Her training, the three months of specialized combat hell Deedee had put her through, snapped into operational reality. Scarlett ripped the comms wire from her shoulder rig—the wire that had just transmitted her agonizing gasp to Arthur—and used the tough plastic insulation to lash her arm tightly above the wound, forming a makeshift tourniquet/pressure bandage. The pain was absolute, driving a low, continuous moan from her chest, but the bleeding slowed.

File Transfer Protocol

She crawled back to the server hub, her body shaking, the floor cold and slick with water from ruptured pipes. She ignored the terror, ignoring the sound of the hostiles regrouping nearby. The transfer bar, that single line of digital truth, was still visible on the screen.

Ten seconds. That's all I need.

She used her non-injured right hand, her fingers flying across the keys, manually bypassing the stalled transfer protocol, forcing the last critical packet of data out to Deedee's secure server. The digital evidence of the Russian OCG's penetration into global banking systems was too valuable to lose.

ACCESS GRANTED. DATA TRANSFER COMPLETE. LOGS WIPED.

The screen flashed the final green confirmation. Scarlett slumped back, the tactical goal achieved. She had won the cyber war; now she had to win the kinetic one.

She shoved herself onto her knees, retrieving the Met-issued P30 pistol she had dropped. The silence was over. She could hear the heavy, tactical boots of the hostiles moving through the corridors—they knew she was wounded, and they knew she was trapped.

The Fight for the Exit

She moved away from the server hub, using the darkness and the acrid chemical smoke that still lingered in the air as her cover. Scarlett's only defense was the evasive combat techniques Arthur had taught her—speed, precise targeting, and exploiting an attacker's balance.

The first man appeared too quickly—a heavy-set figure with a flashlight aimed uselessly high. Scarlett dropped low, exploiting his surprise and his visual blindness. She delivered a savage, precise kick directly to the side of his knee, hearing the gratifying crunch of yielding bone and ligament. He screamed, dropping the flashlight.

The second man was smarter, approaching her position cautiously. Scarlett knew she had to conserve the single magazine Arthur had cited. She used the gun not to shoot, but to hook under his chin, pulling him off balance, slamming him hard against the wall. She disarmed him with a swift twist of the wrist—the technique Arthur had shown her a thousand times on the cottage rug. The man slumped, stunned, his weapon skittering across the floor.

She was exhausted, breathing in heavy, ragged gasps, leaning against the cold concrete for support. Two down. But the exertion was immense. Her left arm was throbbing, a deep, burning ache, and she could taste bile in the back of her throat. She had bought herself seconds, but the cost was nearly total.

A third hostile, moving with terrifying speed, appeared at the end of the corridor. Scarlett raised the pistol, ready to fire the last, necessary round.

Arrival of the Shield

Before she could pull the trigger, the entire far end of the corridor erupted in a deafening, sustained roar of automatic weapon fire. The walls shook, the concrete cracked, and the remaining hostile was instantly driven back, replaced by the terrifying, rhythmic *thud-thud-thud* of highly trained soldiers moving as one unit.

The voice that cut through the noise was raw, precise, and filled with a lethal certainty that could only belong to one man.

"Clear the corridor! Counsel is wounded!"

Scarlett dropped her pistol, the relief making her knees buckle. She was still breathing, she was still standing, and Arthur had come for her. The silence of her own solo war was over.

Chapter 33: Extraction Vector

The noise was absolute—a crushing storm of automatic weapon fire and screaming alarms. Arthur was running, shoving the console aside as the AFO team poured through the breached server hub. He found the AFO team leader (Rhys) securing the immediate area.

"Cover!" Arthur roared, aiming his sidearm toward the far corridor where the remaining hostiles were making a final stand. "Suppressing fire, deep and low!"

He found Scarlett slumped beside the server rack, her face pale, the improvised lashing tight on her arm. Blood pulsed rhythmically through the torn fabric of her jacket.

"Talk to me, Counsel!" Arthur demanded, dropping beside her, ignoring the chaos. He didn't need a diagnosis; he needed functionality.

Scarlett's eyes, though wide with shock, were clear. "Through and through. Left arm. No bone. Transfer complete. They know we won." She pointed to the

AFO team leader. "Rhys gave me two extra clips. Let's move."

Arthur felt the surge of cold pride. She hadn't just survived; she had triaged her own wound and secured replacement assets. *Deedee, you bastard.* The rage over the secret training was deferred; survival was now.

"Rhys, Ben, secure the exit route! Foote, give me live schematic of the ground floor access points!" Arthur dictated over the comms, scooping the operational backpack off the floor and securing the gun in his hand.

The Asset in Action

The escape became a coordinated fight back. Scarlett was weak, her left arm useless, but she was sharp and fast. Arthur used her as a tactical asset, exploiting her small frame and her newly acquired combat training.

"Behind the crates, now!" Arthur commanded, pushing her toward cover.

As two hostiles burst through a fire door, Rhys and Ben engaged them instantly. Arthur kept low, scanning the environment.

"Scarlett! Low-impact, eight o'clock!" Arthur yelled, spotting a mercenary attempting to flank them using a low pipe.

Scarlett didn't hesitate. She launched herself backward, using the server rack for stability, delivering a hard, precise kick that caught the mercenary's kneecap. The man crumpled with a choked cry. Her fighting wasn't powered by strength, but by the trained instinct Arthur himself had perfected—leverage, speed, and exploiting weak points.

Arthur provided cover, firing two precise, disarming shots at the remaining hostile. "Rhys, move up! Ben, secure the exterior!"

The entire Met team was moving in perfect synchronization, treating the extraction not as a retrieval, but as a live deployment with a lethal, highly trained asset.

Clearing the Corridors

The corridors were cleared block by block, the smoke and darkness adding to the confusion. Scarlett, her face set in a grim line, used the pistol with her good hand, quickly mastering the weight and the sight lines. She wasn't just following Arthur; she was maintaining tactical awareness. She emptied the first new clip (provided by Rhys) with disciplined efficiency, targeting shoulders and legs to slow the pursuit without using lethal force—a luxury Arthur couldn't always afford.

Arthur felt the psychological toll of her active participation. He was terrified, watching her duck behind walls, but he was also profoundly aware of her immense capabilities. She wasn't just the woman who needed protection; she was the partner who was securing their exit.

"Last corridor, Arthur! We're hitting the roof access now!" Ben confirmed over the comms.

They reached the roof access point—a heavy fire door leading to the extraction zone. The wind and rain hit them instantly. The roar of the rotors—the Medevac—was deafening.

"One final push, Scarlett! You clear the perimeter!" Arthur yelled over the wind.

Scarlett nodded, her eyes wide with exhaustion, and moved toward the edge of the roof, the pistol held steady in her right hand, securing the perimeter against any hostiles attempting to climb the stairwell.

Arthur sprinted to the Medevac platform, confirming the extraction protocol. He looked back at Scarlett, her body framed against the dark, rainy sky, pistol raised, an image of devastating, capable beauty.

"Go! Go! Go!" Arthur ordered, pulling her onto the platform. The door slammed shut, and the Medevac lifted instantly, leaving the besieged data facility far below.

Arthur collapsed onto the metal floor, pulling Scarlett down with him. The mission was successful. The price of her secret was a bullet wound and a future tied irrevocably to the dangers of the field.

Chapter 34: The Tabulation of Costs

The roar of the Medevac helicopter was a physical pressure, drowning out the frantic noise of the Birmingham data facility far below. Arthur was braced against the metal floor, his entire world centered on the asset—his wife—now lying semi-conscious beneath his field jacket. The mission was successful; the price of success was already being tallied.

Arthur knelt over Scarlett, ignoring the blood soaking his trousers. He carefully sliced away the remains of her tactical jacket, his hands moving with trained, clinical precision, performing the first true assessment of the damage. The improvised lashing on her left arm was crude but effective; the wound was clean, a pass-through that had missed major bone and artery. The danger was blood loss and shock.

"Comms, open secure line to Deedee," Arthur ordered, his voice tight. "Code Sierra. Urgent medical extraction, non-combat. Get a trauma team mobilized at headquarters. I need a clean surgical bay and blood supplies waiting."

He looked at Scarlett. Her eyes were closed, her face pale, but her breathing was steady. She was still holding the pistol. He gently disengaged the weapon from her good hand.

The Betrayal Admitted

Hours later, the Medevac settled onto a secure military airfield outside London. Scarlett was immediately transferred to a clean, heavily secured facility, where professional doctors and nurses took over. Arthur waited, sitting on a folding chair in the sterile corridor, his gaze fixed on the surgical theater door.

He didn't have to wait for the prognosis; he had to wait for the political fallout.

Deedee arrived one hour later, looking immaculate but utterly exhausted. She didn't offer congratulations. She walked straight to Arthur, her expression grim.

"The intelligence is secured," Deedee stated, bypassing pleasantries. "The Russian OCG hub is seized, the data transfer is verified, and the information is critical. You saved the operation, Arthur. You brought her home."

Arthur stood up, his massive frame radiating controlled, lethal disappointment. "You put my wife, less than a year postpartum, in a hostile, live-fire environment. You trained her, armed her, and deployed her without my knowledge. That was a betrayal, Dee. That was a direct violation of protocol and trust."

"It was a directorial mandate," Deedee countered, meeting his gaze without flinching. "Your security profile, your rage, your refusal to accept risk—it made you a liability for deep-cover, institutional access. Scarlett's mind is a unique asset, Arthur. She volunteered. She knew the operational necessity of being unpredictable."

"Operational necessity doesn't override basic human decency," Arthur grated. "The price of your mission was a hole in her arm. And it wasn't even for Gary; it was for a separate Russian threat. That price was too high."

The Consequence of the Lie

Arthur knew the fight was futile. Deedee was the mechanism; the Director was the problem. He accepted the reality: his protective bubble was permanently broken, and his wife was now, irrevocably, an operative in her own right. The Met unit would continue to investigate and act on a spectrum of threats, and she was now a primary resource.

"The unit will provide full coverage for her recovery and protection," Deedee promised, her voice softening slightly. "We are doubling down on the search for Gary and Mr. Harper using the new Radek financial lead. We owe her that much."

Arthur nodded, turning back to the surgical door. "I need full control of her security detail going forward. And I want the name of every operative involved in her training, the facility, and the deployment authorization papers. I need to know every single risk she was exposed to, because I didn't see the danger until it was too late."

Deedee sighed, rubbing her forehead. "I'll get you the file, Arthur. But you need to rest. You look like you're about to collapse."

"I don't rest until the threats are gone," Arthur replied, his voice firm. "The domestic life—the wedding, the stability—that's the final operational goal. And I won't lose that fight."

The wait began. The cost of her secret had been paid, and now Arthur had to process the fact that the woman he loved was both the shield and the sword in the war he was fighting.

Chapter 35: The Cost of the Sword

The first thing Scarlett registered was the absence of pain. Not the distant, managed throb she had grown accustomed to, but a deep, chemically induced numbness that cocooned her body. She was lying in a sterile white bed, the steady rhythm of a monitor confirming her vital signs, the air clean and cold. She was in the secure, clean military facility—the one Deedee had established as the safe haven for high-value assets.

She opened her eyes slowly. Her left arm, heavy and bandaged, was immobilized across her chest. She remembered the searing heat, the crash of the automatic weapon fire, and Arthur's guttural scream as he realized she was hit. The cost was immense. A shallow bullet wound to the non-dominant arm was, thankfully, manageable, but the institutional exposure and the emotional damage to Arthur were the real injuries.

The Unspoken Breach

Arthur sat beside her, asleep in a chair, his face drawn and etched with a profound exhaustion that mirrored her own. When he woke, their conversation was silent for several minutes, conducted entirely in shared memory. She saw the betrayal in his eyes—the rage over her secret training—but beneath it was the absolute relief of her presence.

"I regret the secrecy, Arthur," Scarlett whispered, her throat dry. "I regret the pain the secrecy had caused you."

Arthur shook his head slowly. "You knew I'd veto it. You knew my guilt would blind me. You forced me into a situation where I was irrelevant."

"No," Scarlett countered, her voice gaining strength, despite the effort. "I forced you into a situation where you had to trust the asset. I secured the data, Arthur. I brought down the Russian hub. If I had relied on you to make the decision, I would be on desk duty in Manchester, and that data would be fueling OCGs across Europe. I did my job, Arthur. I did the job you trained me for."

The argument wasn't hostile; it was a necessary debrief, settling the terms of their future partnership.

The Only Way Forward

Deedee entered, carrying a secure tablet and a file. She gave Arthur a brief, weary nod before turning her attention to Scarlett.

"The surgery was clean, Counsel. You'll have limited mobility in that arm for six weeks, but you are structurally sound. The debriefing we ran confirms the intelligence you secured is verified."

Scarlett knew the next step wasn't peace; it was war. She was facing months of grueling physical therapy and a sustained legal fight against Mr. Harper.

"Deedee," Scarlett dictated, "the training continues. The recovery time is now part of the curriculum. I want full access to the surveillance feed on the legal team. We need to anticipate Mr. Harper's final move. And I want to coordinate the asset freezing personally."

Arthur watched, silent. He saw the cold, determined resolve in her eyes. The old Scarlett—the timid solicitor who had feared the chaos of the rave—was gone. The woman before him was the sword he had inadvertently forged.

"I won't lie to you again, Arthur," Scarlett promised, meeting his gaze. "But I will not be sidelined. I am the Counterintelligence Counsel. That job requires me to be competent, not fragile."

Arthur returned to her side, leaning his large frame over the bed. He pressed his lips gently to her forehead, accepting the new terms of their marriage. "We will set the wedding date now, lawyer. We need that legal shield, and we need the stability. But your rehabilitation starts tomorrow. And I am your sole physical therapist."

The fight had fundamentally changed. It was no longer about escaping danger, but about asserting their control over their own lives, together, as two fully engaged operatives. The healing had begun, but the operational commitment was absolute.

Chapter 36: The Last Night of Freedom

Arthur's eyes flashed open. The cold shock of the sheets, the empty space next to him in the bed—it was a visceral alarm. No Scarlett. His head spun instantly toward the baby monitor; Logan was sleeping soundly, the low, even sounds of his breath the only domestic noise.

Where the fuck is she? Panic, cold and absolute, slammed into him, his mind racing, instantly flicking back to the terror of the inn incident. He scrambled out of the bed, not even bothering with his tactical boots, grabbing the secure tablet. The front door was unlocked.

Heart pounding, Arthur had reached the front door, his hand gripping the cold metal, and threw it open.

The Vaping Revelation

The cold night air rushed in, startling Scarlett. She was sat quietly on the rough-hewn woodpile, looking surprisingly small. Jonesy was curled tightly on her lap, a warm, silent confidant against the biting air. She was wearing his thick black coat, its collar pulled high, and between her fingers, a small vape glowed faintly—a soft, pulsing ember against the blackness. The faint scent of bubblegum, oddly sweet and out of place, clung to the air.

"Are you fucking vaping?" Arthur stammered, completely taken back. He was rigid with adrenaline, facing down his worst fear only to be met by a domestic vice.

Scarlett, looking like a deer in the headlights, clearly trying to think of a lie, stuttered before accepting she was caught. "I've vaped for the last eight years, ever since I quit smoking," she admitted, bracing for an argument. "I only do it now if I need to think. And tonight, I needed extreme clarity."

"Think?" Arthur whispered, the concern overriding the anger panicking at the thought she might be changing her mind

"Deedee sent me some documents last night about my dad. I'm worried he's going to try something final, even with the injunction hanging over his head. I needed to run the possibilities," she replied.

She looks so sexy like that, his thoughts surprised him, watching the vape smoke leave her lips and disappear into the frigid air. The mix of total vulnerability and controlled rebellion was devastating.

"Come on, it's fucking baltic out here," she said, standing up, carefully depositing Jonesy onto the woodpile.

"Well, it is November," he replied, his voice still hoarse. He watched her walk ahead, securing the door, and followed her up the stairs. He couldn't help himself from watching the soft sway of her hips as she ascended, the sudden recognition that the fear was gone, replaced by profound, consuming desire. *Christ, this woman has really got me good,* he thought, sliding into bed next to her.

The Final Vow

"How about you help me celebrate my last night of freedom," he chanced, the question heavy with months of suppressed need and the pure relief of the impending ceremony.

"What do you have in mind?" she purred back, clearly understanding the intimate invitation.

Arthur took his chance and pulled her close. He reached down, gripping her hips, and with a powerful surge, he rolled them both, leveraging his strength to pull her up and position her directly astride him.

She shifted, instantly taking complete control of the pace. She then seized the moment, pulling her nightie up over her head, letting the fabric fall away.

Arthur's eyes devoured her body. He tracked the pale lines of her scars—the tight, white stitch mark on her flank, the wound on her arm—each one not a flaw, but a savage symbol of her resilience. The visible history of her trauma only made her more profoundly irresistible. He felt the firm, perfectly toned skin that spoke of her secret combat training, finding the pulse point of their connection.

Arthur devoured the sight of her power. She began to move, slow and deliberate at first, then increasing the speed to a punishing, furious rhythm. She was insatiable, moving with the raw strength of a woman who was finally asserting her right to passion.

Arthur sat himself up, pulling her close, supporting her back with his good arm. He kissed her deeply, completely, the intimacy a final, perfect vow. They were soon pouring with sweat, the heavy, mutual climax serving as the deepest possible commitment to their future.

They just lay there, holding each other for a few minutes, breathing in unison.

"I've really got to get some sleep," Scarlett whispered, finally breaking the silence. "Jade will be here at ten to do my hair and makeup."

"...and Rhys will be here to pick me up at eight to go get readied," Arthur returned, his voice now flat, committed, and ready for the happiest day of his life.

Chapter 37: The Day of the Siege Vow

The cottage was already a hive of quiet, focused activity by 10:00 AM. Jade arrived precisely on time, navigating the AFO security perimeter with practiced ease. The air was cold, carrying the damp, earthy scent of the November moorland, but inside the small cottage, the atmosphere crackled with heat.

Jade, dressed in a stunning emerald dress, immediately took command of the operation. "Right, babe," Jade announced, pulling out a massive case of makeup and hair supplies. "Your job is to sit still, drink this cold prosecco, and try not to cry. My job is to make sure your husband-to-be looks appropriately stunned when you walk down that aisle.".

"If he doesn't cry, you better punch him" Scarlett joked

Scarlett, sitting before the small mirror, laughed, the sound bubbling up from a reservoir of happiness she hadn't known she possessed. The past months—the capture, the trauma, the custody battle, and the constant fear of Mr. Harper's litigation—had been a dark apprenticeship. Today was the culmination of that fight.

The Unveiling

The dress hung carefully secured on the bedroom door, hidden from Arthur's protective eyes. It was a magnificent contradiction, exactly fitting the journey they had shared. Jade finally unveiled it with a dramatic flourish.

The top was a beautifully structured corset, laced tightly but delicately with satin ribbon, a deliberate and striking nod back to the rave where they first met. The intricate beading sewn across the bodice caught the light, flowing down into a curve-hugging satin skirt that emphasized the beautiful, hard-won shape of her postpartum body. The gown trailed into a long, detailed train that pooled dramatically on the cottage floor. Over her shoulders lay a generous shawl of faux white fur, a practical shield against the Peak air, symbolizing the protection Arthur had wrapped around her.

"It's breathtaking," Scarlett whispered, touching the soft satin.

"It is defiance," Jade corrected, tears welling up. "It's a warrior's dress. Now, get in it."

The ritual of dressing was slow, intimate, and emotional. Jade secured the final laces, pulling the corset tight, and secured the beautiful, shimmering veil into the intricate updo she had created with Scarlett's dark hair. The veil transformed the look, shifting the defiance into something ethereal and pure.

Logan, completely oblivious to the operational significance of the day, was dressed next. Arthur had chosen a miniature, perfect black tux, complete with a tiny waistcoat and bow tie. Logan looked like a tiny, extremely serious bodyguard.

Operation First Look

At precisely 12:45 PM, a car horn sounded—a deep, resonant rumble that meant the final extraction team was ready. Ben, Arthur's quiet, pragmatic AFO team-mate, had drawn the coveted job of driving the bride.

Scarlett adjusted the shawl and took a final, deep breath. The front door opened, and Ben stood there, looking profoundly uncomfortable in a tailored suit. Behind him, parked on the muddy track, was his vehicle—a gleaming, classic red Mustang, polished to a mirror shine.

"Mrs. Jacobs," Ben said, his voice husky. "The transport is ready."

He helped carry the heavy gown and Logan's car seat. Ben secured Logan's car seat in the front passenger seat (safe due to the older model's lack of airbags). Logan, now a fully dressed miniature operative, was positioned securely.

Ben leaned close to Scarlett and tapped his secure comms unit. "Route code confirmed. Operation Valkyrie," he whispered, a grim smile touching his lips.

Scarlett stepped back, her hand resting on the fabric of the elaborate dress. "You tell Arthur absolutely nothing about this dress. Don't ruin the surprise. We need the full impact."

Ben grinned, saluting mockingly with his comms unit. "*Foote, copy that. Valkyrie is en route to target. The assets are secure, and my lips are sealed.*"

The Final Aisle

The short drive was tense, blending the ordinary journey with the extraordinary weight of the consequences. They reached St. Stephen's Church, Hassop, the ancient stone chapel sitting stoically against the backdrop of the grey hills. The external security was invisible but absolute: Rhys and his perimeter team were already in position.

Ben gently helped Scarlett out of the Mustang, careful not to snag the elaborate train. He offered his arm. He would walk her down the aisle, a silent commitment to Arthur's safety.

The music started inside the chapel—a slow, classic melody. The heavy oak doors swung open.

Scarlett stepped onto the threshold, the cold November light illuminating the beautiful cascade of her veil and train. She walked slowly, absorbing the sight of the small, vetted congregation.

Her eyes locked immediately on Arthur. He stood rigid at the altar, his broad shoulders squared in the tailored suit, his professional armor impenetrable until he saw her.

The moment he did, the armor shattered. His intense brown eyes widened, glistening instantly with unshed tears, the sudden, profound rush of relief and love overwhelming his soldier's control.

Beside him, Rhys let out a short, surprised laugh, a sharp, necessary sound that broke the spell of the room, and he clapped his best friend firmly on the back.

Scarlett walked forward, her heart filled with a triumphant, quiet roar. The wedding was a battlefield, but she was walking toward the only peace she had ever known.

Chapter 38: The Vow Interrupted

The small chapel in the Peak District was hushed, the only sounds the solemn notes of the acoustic melody and the soft movement of the winter light through the stained glass. Arthur stood rigid at the altar, his entire focus consumed by the open doorway. Rhys, impeccably dressed as best man, stood beside him, occasionally offering a subtle check on the internal security positions.

He saw her. Scarlett. She was breathtaking—a vision of defiant beauty in a simple white silk dress, the corset bodice a stark reminder of the chaotic night they met. The river stone ring, the symbol of their chaotic, absolute love, rested on her finger.

The professional armor Arthur wore disintegrated instantly. He saw not the Counterintelligence Counsel, but his wife, the mother of his son, walking toward the peace they had fought so savagely to earn. His intense brown eyes widened, glistening instantly with unshed tears, the profound rush of relief and love overwhelming his soldier's control. Beside him, Rhys clapped his best friend firmly on the back, a sharp, necessary sound that acknowledged the emotion.

Code Black: The 30-Man Breach

Scarlett was halfway down the aisle when the moment shattered.

The heavy oak doors at the back of the chapel burst inward with the controlled, violent efficiency of a mass breach. The sound was loud, tearing through the music. Two men in sharp, dark suits—their demeanor screaming high-level NCA/MI5—strode purposefully down the aisle. They were flanked by four massive men in unmarked tactical gear, their weapons held at low ready.

The chapel immediately devolved into a chaotic operational zone. Rhys and Ben moved instantly, drawing weapons, hands flashing inside their jackets. The entire congregation of vetted operatives, excluding only civilian partners and children, rose as one, engaging the overwhelming numbers.

The fight was immediate and brutal. Arthur's fury was a cold, internal fire. He deployed instantly, engaging the two closest hostile agents who had peeled off the main assault column to secure the altar. Arthur's movements were swift and lethal, fueled by adrenaline.

Scarlett was tackled by four agents near the front of the aisle. She kicked, twisted, and fought with the full repertoire of the close-quarters combat Arthur had taught her, forcing the agents to use severe restraint to finally subdue her.

The melee consumed the nave. A cloud of non-lethal, high-impact gas was deployed by the hostile team, confusing the front rank of the Met operatives. Rhys and Ben were locked in desperate hand-to-hand combat with the tactical guards.

The Unstoppable Lie

It was only then, as the brawl escalated, that two men in sharp, dark suits—the negotiators—strode purposefully past the main fighting, unaffected by the incapacitant gas, heading straight for Deedee.

The lead suit reached Deedee, tossing a sealed document toward her. "Detective Inspector Hayes. This is a sealed judicial order and a warrant signed by the

High Court. Conspiracy and Obstruction of Justice. Order your men to stand down, or we will escalate force."

Deedee snatched the document, scanning the dense legal text and the judicial seal. Her face went white with the devastating realization. This wasn't a crude ambush; this was a legally sanctioned operation. The warrant was flawless, citing Conspiracy and Obstruction of Justice under the pretense of national security.

"Stand down! Stand down, now!" Deedee roared into her comms, the sound echoing the institutional failure. "They are legitimate! Weapons secured!"

Rhys and Ben, stunned, broke off the fight, their own guns slowly lowered. Rhys and one AFO immediately had to restrain Arthur, whose rage became a violent, physical need to reach Scarlett.

The Final Isolation

The suited agents, now victorious, hauled Scarlett back up the aisle, ignoring Arthur's struggles.

"What the fuck has she done?!" Arthur screamed, struggling wildly against Rhys's grip. "She works for the government, for Christ's sake!"

The lead agent stopped beside Arthur. He ignored the outburst, speaking coldly to Scarlett. "You are under arrest. You will remain silent."

"Oh, this is utter bullshit! Let me see the fucking paper!" Scarlett shouted, her voice raw, demanding her legal rights even as she was being dragged away.

In the commotion, Logan, who was being held safely by Jade near a side exit, began to scream for his mother.

Deedee ran to the aisle, tears streaming down her face. "We'll fight this, Scarlett! We'll get you out! Just sit tight!"

The agents hauled Scarlett through the shattered oak doors. Her veil was askew, her dress ripped slightly at the shoulder.

Arthur watched the final, devastating image: his bride, in handcuffs and a white wedding dress, was gone.

He was left restrained and immobilized, his family publicly shattered, realizing the betrayal was institutional, and the fight for the Ledger's Toll had just begun again.

Chapter 39: The Vanishing Bride

The clang of the heavy oak doors shutting behind Scarlett marked the violent end of her wedding and the final, crushing victory of the authorities. She was seized immediately by the hostile agents, the illusion of the NCA/MI5 authority dissolving the instant they had her secured. She was still in her white wedding dress, the fragile silk ripped slightly at the shoulder, with the metal handcuffs flashing ironically against the white lace.

She was bundled roughly—but with professional care—into the back of a large, unmarked black van. Four massive men in tactical gear immediately surrounded her, weapons held at low ready. They treated her not like a captured witness, but like a lethal, caged threat.

Her initial, operational fury was replaced by a cold, absolute resolve. She refused to look at the men, focusing instead on the agonizing sound of Logan's cries receding into the distance—a sound that was instantly shut off by the solid steel of the van door.

The Tactical Transit

The drive was high-speed and relentless, lasting approximately thirty minutes. Scarlett felt the van weave aggressively through the countryside roads, relying on speed and professional driving to escape the immediate area. The silence in the back was broken only by the sharp, clipped communication of the four mercenaries, all speaking in low, unrecognizable dialects.

Two men sat directly opposite Scarlett, their weapons—heavy, suppressed assault rifles—trained on her chest with unwavering, professional focus. The two others sat flanking her, their hands ready. Scarlett felt their intense, calculated scrutiny. They were treating her like a highly dangerous asset, or a velociraptor—a creature too valuable to harm, yet too lethal to ignore.

She tried to engage the lead mercenary, testing the perimeter. "You're making a mistake," Scarlett stated, her voice hoarse. "That warrant is flawed. When the Met finds out you've taken a Counterintelligence Counsel..."

The man merely shifted his rifle and stared, his face a neutral mask beneath the low light of the van's cabin. "We are only following the law, Miss Harper. Your security classification is paramount." His complete lack of emotion was chilling.

The psychological warfare was effective. She realized they were driven by a contract that superseded local loyalties. Her only hope was that Arthur would correctly prioritize the Met's operational resources to locate her final destination.

The Air Transfer

The van eventually stopped. The doors were wrenched open, plunging the back into cold, dim light. Before Scarlett could even assess the environment, a thick, heavy black bag was pulled roughly over her head. The world instantly became suffocating, disorienting noise.

She was lifted violently—the surprising effort of the mercenary lifting her confirming the sheer number of tactical layers they were employing. She felt the rush of cold air and the immediate, rising whine of a turbine engine. She was being put into a helicopter. The sound vibration was immense, traveling through the rough fabric of the bag and deep into her bones.

The air travel was lengthy and brutal, designed purely to erase her sense of direction and time. She felt the pitch and yaw of the chopper, trying desperately to use her internal clock to gauge the distance, but the effort was futile. She was moving to a deeply secure, highly isolated location.

The Final Prison

The noise finally subsided. She was dragged out, her feet stumbling on rough concrete. The bag was ripped from Scarlett's head. She blinked rapidly against the sudden, cold glare. She was in a small, windowless concrete cell, brightly lit, cold, and utterly sterile. It smelled of fresh paint, bleach, and institutional abandonment. Her wrists were immediately shoved into heavy metal handcuffs and secured to an old, heavy steel interrogation table bolted to the floor, forcing her into an awkward, painful posture. She was stripped of her shoes, leaving her exposed and vulnerable.

She scanned the environment, noting the single, reinforced door and the lack of windows. The helplessness of being restrained after fighting so fiercely was crushing. She was back in the familiar landscape of her greatest trauma. *I need to find the legal angle,* she thought, forcing her mind away from the panic. *The warrant—it had to be the Contempt charge.*

The heavy steel door to the cell hissed open.

A figure stood silhouetted against the bright light of the corridor. He walked in, impeccably dressed, looking completely calm and utterly victorious.

"Welcome home, Scarlett," Mr. Harper said, his voice echoing in the concrete room, a low, cold thunder that brought the whole terrible reality crashing down. "Let's discuss the immediate withdrawal of that defense motion."

Chapter 40: The Institutional Void

The stillness in St. Stephen's Chapel was deafening, suffocating. It had been several minutes since the heavy oak doors crashed shut, taking Scarlett with them. Arthur was released from Rhys's restraint, staggering to the altar. The scene was now a forensic tableau: overturned pews, scattered rose petals, and the empty space where his bride had stood.

Deedee, already on a secure satellite line, was marshaling her team, her face grim, managing the immediate crisis.

Arthur ignored the chaos. He walked to the vestry, retrieved his tactical pack—which contained the stolen pistol—and walked back to the center of the chapel.

Deedee was on the phone, using the highest clearance scramble codes. "*MI5 Command, this is Met DI Hayes. I need immediate confirmation on a high-risk operation executed at St. Stephen's Church, Hassop. Warrant status: Conspiracy and Obstruction of Justice. Agents: Six, unmarked tactical. Who authorized this extraction?*"

The answer, filtered through the secure comms, was immediate and devastatingly clear: No one.

Deedee slammed the handset down, her face drawn. "It's fake," she stated, the devastating truth echoing in the small chapel. "The warrant was forged. The signatures are false. They were mercenaries."

The Unraveling and the New Threat

Arthur ignored the financial detail, his focus fixed on the single truth: "They were mercs, Dee. They were a hostile team."

He turned instantly toward Jade, who was desperately trying to soothe the crying Logan. Arthur gently lifted his son, settling the small, trembling body against his chest, transferring the role of primary security back to himself.

"He's gone to ground," Arthur stated, his voice flat, devoid of emotion, addressed to Deedee. "He used a false warrant and official uniforms. He knows the Clock is ticking, and he knows the Met's operational response time is tied up by bureaucracy and political risk."

"*Arthur, we need to consider the full threat,*" Deedee countered, her voice now thick with exhaustion. "*We don't know who funded the warrants—it could be Gary's final play, or it could be the Russians, using this moment to settle old scores. We need your testimony to validate the evidence.*"

Arthur shook his head slowly, looking past her, his gaze fixed on the broken doorway. "The institution failed, Dee. It failed because it was too slow to act on the truth, and it failed because it honored a lie. I'm not waiting for a political solution. I'm taking the threat to the field."

"If you go rogue, Arthur," Deedee warned, her voice rising, "*you become a genuine fugitive. You lose all institutional protection.*"

"I lost my protection when I let my bride be handcuffed," Arthur countered. "The Met's goal is to clean up a treason case. My goal is to retrieve my wife and end the man who took her. I'm going off-book."

His first priority was security. He walked to the side exit where Rhys and Ben stood, overseeing the packing of the forensic equipment.

Arthur pulled out his phone, accessing the tactical tracking grid. He opened the app for the covert trackers, the screen a blank void until a second later. He didn't breathe. He was risking the final failure on a desperate hope: that Scarlett, true to her nature, had worn her old Converse under the wedding dress as her "something old." To his profound relief, the hope was justified. A single, tenacious green dot glowed on the map, stationary in the middle of the capital.

"Dee," Arthur stated, his voice now dangerously calm, holding the phone steady while continuing to rock Logan. "If I give you a precise, verifiable location for the asset, will that give me the resources and support to run a clean extraction?"

Deedee stared at the phone, seeing the live dot. "*Where is she, Arthur?*"

"She's at Harper's office in London. He took her straight to the center of his legal operation."

The Final Mobilization

Arthur spent a final, agonizing hour coordinating the handoff. He kissed Logan, tracing the small curve of his son's cheek, imprinting the feeling of his warmth. He handed the now-quieted child to Rhys.

"Deedee," Arthur stated, moving to the escape car. "I'm taking the vehicle. I want access to the Met's international flight logs and a private signal bounce off the French coast. I'm calling in all my favors, and I'm going completely dark."

"You'll get the support you need," Deedee vowed, meeting him by the car. "But you're on your own, Arthur. No rules, no backup beyond what you recruit. Just you and your target."

Arthur climbed into the driver's seat. He looked back at the cold stone chapel, at his friends surrounding the quiet miracle of his son, and at the devastation left behind by a piece of paper. He started the engine, the low hum a stark contrast to the roar of the earlier brawl. The wedding was over. The rescue had begun.

Chapter 41: The Patriarch's Prison

The heavy steel door hissed shut behind Mr. Harper, isolating Scarlett completely. She was a devastating vision of captivity: her white silk wedding dress, now crumpled and torn slightly at the shoulder, contrasted brutally with the cold, raw metal of the handcuffs securing her wrists to the steel interrogation table. The concrete cell was small, bright, and smelled of disinfectant—a clinical environment designed for mental, not physical, duress.

Mr. Harper did not sit on the adjacent stool. He stood, towering over her, his expression a mixture of profound, cold contempt and managerial annoyance.

"Thousands of pounds and political capital expended today, Scarlett," Mr. Harper began, his voice a low, precise thunder. "All because you couldn't resist a common urge to commit an act of defiance. The wedding was a beautiful, public display of utter contempt for my authority and your legal standing."

Scarlett didn't flinch, despite the strain in her arms and the chill of the metal against her wrists. Her fury had hardened into a cold, diamond-like point. "You smug bastard," she spat, aiming for maximum personal damage. "Your mercenary shot a civilian, hijacked a church, and forged a High Court warrant! The charges against you—treason, criminal conspiracy—are now irrevocable."

Mr. Harper merely smoothed the lapel of his expensive suit, dismissing the charges as vulgar administrative errors. "Gary is an unfortunate necessity, Scarlett. His methods are crude, but his influence is useful. That, however, is immaterial to your immediate problem. The arrest, while tactically messy, was legally perfect. You are now facing contempt charges for defying a judicial injunction."

The Operational Damage Report

"Your position is simple," Mr. Harper continued, walking slowly around the table, forcing her eyes to follow him. "The Ledger is secure with the Met, but I need to know precisely what digital damage you inflicted on my financial systems after you digitized the file. You will immediately sign an affidavit withdrawing the Tainted

Evidence motion you filed, and you will agree to undo any damage you caused while hacking my servers."

"And why would I do that?"

"Because your value lies in your mind," Mr. Harper sneered. "I need you on my side, managing the legal defense, and securing my operations. You will use your expertise to lock down every file Arthur ever saw and begin hacking my competitors."

"You have no grounds for custody," Scarlett countered, shifting in the heavy, white dress. "The French marriage is valid. We are legally protected."

"The French marriage," Mr. Harper corrected, his voice dripping with condescension, "was performed under duress, without proper disclosure, and is an active target of a civil appeal. It is currently ambiguous. Your compliance is Logan's safety."

The Logan Lever

Scarlett realized the true nature of her father's visit. This wasn't about love; it was about the Ledger and the control over her unique skills.

"You want me to lock down the digital file you thought was safe," she deduced, her voice sharp despite the physical restraint. "You want me to erase the forensic footprints that I left on the systems. You're afraid of the Met's digital evidence."

Mr. Harper smiled—a terrifying expression of business self-interest. "I am afraid of your *ingenuity*, dear. You are, after all, my daughter. You used the finest education money could buy to become a traitor. Now you will use that mind to secure my assets."

He leaned in close, his scent—expensive cologne and old paper—suffocating. "Go to hell, Dad," Scarlett hissed, her voice shaking with rage. "You think you can bully me with a forged warrant and a family trust fund? You lost me the day you chose your ledger over your blood."

"You have two days to consider the proposal. If you choose defiance, your continued association with Detective Jacobs will be used to finalize the custody order. I will take my grandson, raise him correctly, and ensure you never see him again. Think of your mother, Scarlett. She would have wanted stability for her grandson."

Mr. Harper stepped back, nodding toward the heavy steel door. "When you are ready to withdraw the Tainted Evidence motion and secure the Ledger, the security detail will inform me."

The door hissed open, and Mr. Harper strode out, leaving Scarlett alone. She didn't struggle against the cuffs. She felt the chill of the concrete floor and the terrifying, cold dread of the knowledge: her father held the highest ground, controlling not only the courts but also her child's future. She started working through the complex legal jargon in her mind, searching for the crack in the institutional lie. The fight was still on.

Chapter 42: The North Sea Pursuit

Arthur's heart hammered against his ribs. He was driving—a sanctioned detective sergeant, commanding a retrieval operation supported entirely by the uncompromised fraction of the Met (Deedee/Foote). The devastation of the wedding was fresh, raw, and absolute.

His initial fury had settled into a cold, diamond-hard focus. He reviewed the tactical situation: Scarlett was being held at Mr. Harper's private office in the capital's financial district—a location confirmed by the live Converse tracker. He had to breach the location *now*, before she disappeared again.

Arthur drove straight to a pre-arranged rendezvous point outside the city with Rhys and Ben.

Tactical Mobilization

The meet was fast and professional. Ben and Rhys, grim-faced and exhausted, were already there with additional gear.

"Logan is secure with Emily," Rhys reported, his eyes sweeping the perimeter. "Jade is with them. They're safe, Arthur. Your worry is here."

"The target is the financial district," Arthur stated, pulling out the building blueprints Deedee had forwarded from a remote server. "Thirty-six stories. High security. We're hitting the private access floor, ten minutes pre-dawn. We hit the security hub, neutralize the perimeter, and extract Scarlett."

Arthur's plan was simple and relied on extreme speed. They were kitted out in low-profile, dark tactical gear that allowed maximum mobility. Ben, the technician, would handle the initial penetration and the internal comms relay. Rhys, the security specialist, would cover the entry and set up the escape route. Arthur would take the primary assault role.

"We need to assume Mr. Harper has armed protection," Arthur instructed. "These aren't local beat cops anymore. They're professionals paid to guard the evidence."

"We're betting on the clock," Ben noted. "They're expecting the police to move legally, not an immediate, armed retrieval. Surprise is our only asset."

The Empty Room and the Trap

The breach of the external security was textbook. They bypassed the main lobby and took the service elevator upward.

Arthur moved through the pristine, silent corridors of the financial firm, the contrast between the wealth and the violence of the situation jarring. They reached the floor identified as Mr. Harper's private archive.

The door was reinforced steel. Ben moved quickly, deploying a specialized optic probe. "*Three heat signatures inside, Arthur. Two guards, one stationary—Harper.*"

"On my mark," Arthur whispered into the comms. "Three... two... one. Go!"

The charge blew the hinges cleanly. Arthur burst through the door, weapon ready. He found the room instantly. It was the same concrete holding cell, the same steel interrogation table—but it was empty.

The Converse tracker—the single green dot he had followed with absolute faith—was lying in the middle of the floor, the wire cleanly clipped. It was a trap.

Arthur's world dissolved into pure, cold fury. He was too late. He had traded his wife's freedom for a tracker that had been used to lure him into the financial district.

Rhys moved instantly, neutralizing two guards who were scrambling toward a hidden alarm panel. Arthur ignored the prone figures and moved straight toward the fourth heat signature—Mr. Harper's handler, who was attempting to escape via a rear exit.

Phase Delta: Interrogation and New Vector

Arthur, bypassing any standard judicial procedure, grabbed the captured merc by the throat and slammed him against a wall of archived legal documents. "Where is she? Where did they take her?" Arthur demanded, his voice dangerously low.

The mercenary, terrified by the sheer, unbridled rage of the man in the tactical gear, broke immediately. He spoke quickly, pointing toward a shipping manifest on a secure desk.

"The docks... she's on a high-speed ferry, sir! Hook of Holland! Rotterdam! It left hours ago! Mr. Harper's transferring her to his main holding facility in the Netherlands! They took her to stop the court order!"

Arthur released the man, the terror replaced by a renewed, icy focus. Rotterdam. A new country, a new sea crossing, and a whole new set of jurisdictional nightmares.

Hours later, the London office was secured, the captured mercenary was handed off to Deedee's clean team for debriefing.

"Deedee, I need immediate confirmation on the manifest for the ferry to Rotterdam. Mobilize everything," Arthur dictated into the comms. "The war has moved to the North Sea."

The Maritime Contingency

The planning shifted entirely to a maritime intercept. The ferry was already miles ahead, but Mr. Harper's team would be traveling under civilian cover, making them vulnerable.

"Foote confirms a large, privately owned, high-speed coastal patrol vessel, the *Resolution*, is available," Deedee reported. "It's clean. You'll be crossing the North Sea in a comms blackout."

Arthur nodded, already formulating the final legal/personal maneuver. He contacted the skipper of the *Resolution* directly. "Captain. I need a massive favor. We're intercepting an asset transfer on a North Sea commercial route. I need your speed, and I need absolute radio silence. We need to secure the legal shield against Mr. Harper's final attacks."

The Captain, a gruff Scotsman, paused. "*Aye, I understand the stakes, Jacobs. I'll be ready.*"

Arthur gathered his team. Rhys and Ben secured the necessary equipment—breaching gear, additional non-lethal suppressive weapons, and marine climbing apparatus. The objective was no longer land-based; it was a dark, dangerous approach across the North Sea.

They boarded the *Resolution*. The engines roared to life, cutting through the swells. Arthur was standing in the bow, the sea spray hitting his face, the Ledger secure at Met HQ, and his future sailing toward him across the choppy water.

The intercept was set. The final, high-stakes confrontation would take place at dawn, somewhere halfway between Britain and the Hook of Holland.

Chapter 43: The Cut and The Climb

The continuous, low drone of the ship's engines throbbed through the floor, a constant, unsettling lullaby. Scarlett was sealed in what she assumed to be a junior officer's cabin on the fast maritime vessel. The room was clearly lived in, containing personal items and framed photos scattered throughout—but nothing that could serve as a weapon or aid in escape. The only source of light was a single ceiling lamp, swaying slightly with the choppy North Sea.

"Great," Scarlett thought, the words bitter and exhausted. "Another fucking boat."

She was still in her wedding dress, now utterly destroyed. The white silk was crumpled and stained, the long train black and torn from being dragged across the docks during her brutal journey. Beads were missing from her corset bodice, which was still laced tight, and her veil had been confiscated after she'd made a desperate, unsuccessful attempt to strangle one of the mercs with it during the helicopter transfer.

Despair, cold and heavy, was settling over her. They had found the sophisticated tracker in her Converse—their final, tactical line of communication. *How the hell was Arthur going to find her now, knowing only that she was somewhere over the North Sea?*

The Escape Protocol

She slipped her hand into the neck of her dress and retrieved the small vape she had managed to stash in her bra, relieved they hadn't found it when searching her for weapons. She drew a slow, deep breath, the sweet bubblegum flavor cutting through the fear. Puffing away like a chain smoker, Scarlett's formidable analytical brain began working.

Her primary obstacle was mobility. She moved to the dresser mirror, twisting to survey the ruins of her gown. *If I have to run, this dress will drown me.* With a sudden, fierce resolve, she grabbed the bottom of the elaborate silk skirt and tore the fabric, ripping it cleanly to the knee. She grabbed the long, torn train, which represented the formal, failed vow, and pulled it free, discarding the useless silk onto the polished mahogany floor. The act was both practical and symbolic—shedding the lie of her perfect wedding.

Next, the lock. She examined the heavy door and its brass latch. It was an old-fashioned mechanism, not a digital keypad. She reached up, pulling two bobby pins from the elaborate updo Jade had painstakingly crafted. Her father, long ago, had told her that the oldest tricks were always the best.

Ignoring the pain in her aching back and legs, Scarlett knelt by the door. Her hands, despite their initial tremor, became steady. She inserted the pins, working with the focused concentration she usually reserved for complex legal contracts or coding injections. The minutes stretched, slow and taut. Finally, with a soft, mechanical *click*, the lock yielded. A profound surge of defiance and triumph pulsed through her.

The Unplanned Jump

Scarlett gently opened the cabin door. The narrow corridor was empty, smelling faintly of fuel and salt air. She slipped out, the shorter skirt of her wedding dress providing the necessary freedom of movement. She moved silently, relying on the evasive training Arthur had taught her—using the gentle sway of the ship to mask her footsteps.

Her intention was absolute: find the highest point, jump, and take her chances in the frigid North Sea. Drowning was preferable to becoming her father's ultimate tool.

She made it two decks up, nearing the main observation level, when the confrontation began. Two heavily armed mercenaries emerged from a service stairwell, carrying plastic containers.

Scarlett didn't wait to be challenged. Her body, trained for aggression, moved instantly. She closed the distance with startling speed, exploiting the narrow corridor. She delivered a lightning-fast kick, leveraging her weight to hit the closest merc behind the knee. He staggered, dropping his container with a crash. As the second merc spun, she used the edge of the corridor wall to rebound, driving her elbow hard into his solar plexus. The men crumpled instantly, neutralized by her sheer, focused surprise and agility.

She stood panting over the two incapacitated figures, tasting the metallic tang of adrenaline. She grabbed the discarded service pistol from one of the mercenaries.

The silence that followed was ripped apart, not by a challenge from below, but by a sound that vibrated the very structure of the ship: the sustained, rapid roar of automatic weapon fire erupting from the bridge level directly above her.

Arthur was here. The final fight had just begun.

Chapter 44: The Mid-Ocean Vow

The small patrol boat, the *Resolution*, was a speck of black steel fighting the immense, choppy churn of the North Sea. The pre-dawn light was weak, filtering through a thick marine fog. Arthur was hunched in the bow, the sea spray freezing instantly on his gear. The silhouette of the target—a massive, converted cargo ferry bound for Rotterdam—loomed ahead, a colossal black shadow churning across the water.

The Scottish captain, a gruff, silent genius, proved his worth instantly. He maneuvered the small vessel with uncanny skill, placing the *Resolution* directly against the bouncing, unforgiving metal stern of the ferry. The sea was fighting him, throwing the small boat violently against the hull, but the Captain held it steady.

"Theres a lot of people on there, mate," Rhys warned over the comms, his voice grim as he reviewed the infrared feed. "At least a hundred chaps. That's a full OCG deployment."

"One hundred to three," Ben breathed, checking the breach gear. "Fuck it, Arthur. This is suicide. We hit the engine room first."

Arthur felt the cold, familiar clarity of extreme danger. He looked at his friends. "You both have families, I don't expect you to come with me. It's suicide."

Rhys shook his head, pulling his massive GPMG (General Purpose Machine Gun) into position. "We're family too, Arthur. And one of ours is on that boat. I'm with you." Ben nodded, securing his MP5.

"We do this then," Arthur whispered, a profound gratitude overriding the terror.

The Assault on the Hull

They moved with brutal efficiency. Ben threw the grapple, the steel hook biting into the cold metal of the ferry's stern rail. Arthur was the first up, scaling the rope ladder with a fierce, burning speed, his good arm pulling his full body weight and gear. Rhys and Ben followed, their equipment—MP5s, pistols, flashbangs, and the heavy GPMG gifted by Foote—slung over their shoulders.

They silently climbed over the side onto the main vehicle deck. The vast, empty space smelled of diesel and salt. Arthur spared a quick look back; the *Resolution* had already slipped away into the dark swell behind the ferry, leaving them completely isolated.

"Mate, no matter which door we pick it's a shit show," Rhys hissed, checking the infrared again. "No clear path to the bridge. We go central, take the stairs."

The infiltration was textbook until they hit the main administration stairwell. The alarm was sounded instantly—a piercing, high-pitched wail that transformed the silent vessel into an active warzone.

Pinned on the Bridge

The bridge access door was locked. Ben deployed the cutting torch, the sudden, deafening whine of the plasma cutter masking the sound of incoming fire.

They burst onto the bridge—a wide, glass-fronted room filled with navigation consoles and equipment. Gary was gone, having slipped away seconds before the breach. But waiting for them was a heavy contingent of hostile security.

Arthur's team was instantly pinned down behind the steel navigation consoles. But the shock of the hostile fire was immediate—it wasn't just directed *at* them.

Arthur looked up and saw the impossible. Scarlett was already fighting.

She was positioned behind the main steering column, her white wedding dress ripped at the skirt for mobility. Her face was grim, her dark hair was matted with sweat, and she was bloodied from battle and flying wood. She was firing a service pistol she had secured on the vessel, alongside the terrified ship's captain, who was desperately returning fire with a shotgun. Her advanced training had kicked in, turning the bridge into a makeshift defense post.

"It's a two-sided fight!" Ben roared, slamming suppressive fire toward the main corridor.

The firefight was deafening, the bridge a maelstrom of destruction. Bullets slammed into the consoles, ricocheting about their heads, the wooden panels splintering into lethal shrapnel around them. They were completely surrounded by mercenary fire from the corridors and the catwalks above.

Arthur watched his wife, now a fully deployed operative, emptying her clip into the enemy. The raw, beautiful strength of her commitment was absolute.

The sound of the battle dissolved again. Arthur was in slow motion, his world reduced to the sight of her face, confirming she was whole and fighting. *Shit, this is it,* he thought, *we made it this far, only to die on this ship.*

He noticed the Captain huddled just along from them, his shotgun barrel smoking. Arthur knew he had to secure the legal shield before the inevitable end.

"I need five seconds!" Arthur yelled, diving across the floor, reaching Scarlett. He grabbed her hand, pulling her toward him.

"I can't stop shooting!" Scarlett shouted, reloading her pistol with practiced, quick efficiency.

Arthur ignored the practical impossibility of the situation. "Captain! I need you now!" he demanded, pointing his pistol toward the enemy, then back toward the terrified man. "MARRY US! NOW!"

The Captain, terrified, stammered, "W-what? Are you fucking serious? I'm covering my head from the splinters!"

"NOW!" Arthur roared, firing two precise, disarming shots towards the catwalk. He felt a sudden, sharp, hot pain tear through his left arm—a bullet grazing him. Scarlett, instantly focused, dropped her weapon and scrambled to put pressure on the wound with a piece of her ruined dress.

"If I'm dying, I'm dying a married man!" Arthur bellowed, his voice straining against the gunfire and his own adrenaline.

The Captain, seeing the blood and the absolute resolve, complied instantly. He performed the ceremony in a rushed, frantic voice, the words of the legal vow interspersed with the deafening sound of gunfire and splintering wood.

Arthur looked into Scarlett's eyes, speaking his commitment while his world disintegrated. He confirmed the words. "I do."

"And you, Ms. Harper?" the Captain yelled.

"I do!" she shouted, clutching his arm, confirming the final, irreversible vow.

Arthur pulled her against his chest, their kiss brief, fierce, and absolute.

The words were instantly cut off by a tremendous, deafening EXPLOSION somewhere deep within the ship's hull. The deck beneath them bucked violently. The sound of twisting, groaning metal replaced the gunfire.

The ship was sinking. The wedding was sealed. The game had just changed for good.

Chapter 45: Sinking Protocol

The world ended in the sound of twisting, groaning metal. The tremendous, deafening explosion deep within the ferry's hull—the cost of Mr. Harper's final, desperate attempt to eliminate the evidence—sent the bridge bucking violently. Arthur, gripping Scarlett tight, felt the entire deck beneath them lurch and list sharply to the port side. Water alarms shrieked instantly, adding a new, piercing layer to the chaos.

"Ben! Rhys! Status!" Arthur roared, scrambling to secure his footing behind the steel consoles. He was now officially a married man, but the honeymoon was the North Sea.

"*We're taking fire! Ship's sinking! The stairs are compromised!*" Rhys yelled over the comms, already setting up suppressive fire to cover the main corridor exit. "*Bulkhead doors are flooding!*"

Arthur didn't need confirmation. The water streaming down the bridge windows and the severe list meant the vessel was going down fast.

"Captain, damage report!" Arthur snapped at the terrified man, who was clinging to the wheel. "Escape route! Where is the nearest clear exit to the lifeboats?"

The Descent into Hell

The escape was a terrifying, violent scramble down the compromised decks. Arthur, Rhys, and Ben were fighting against two enemies: the collapsing structure and the remaining mercenaries who were now panicked, firing wildly, trying to secure their own exit.

Arthur led the way, covering the rear. As they moved down the main stairwell, a burst of hostile fire slammed into the group. Rhys cried out, his left shoulder absorbing a grazing round. Ben took a similar graze to his right flank. Both men shrugged off the pain, treating the wounds as a necessary tax on the mission. They exchanged fire, neutralizing the mercs and pushing forward.

Arthur took his second hit near the mid-deck access—a round tearing through his already compromised right shoulder. The pain was immense, making his good arm nearly useless for his heavy weapon. He dropped his MP5, relying solely on his sidearm and pure rage.

Scarlett, despite the terror, was immediately operational. She secured the Captain, forcing the frightened man to lead them through the chaotic, listing corridors. She still clutched the pistol, moving with controlled, brutal efficiency.

"Scarlett, cover! They're coming hard!"

Scarlett turned instantly, firing three precise shots that drove the pursuit back. She was bloodied, exhausted, and now seeing her husband disabled.

The Final Sacrifice

They reached the lower vehicle deck. The listing was severe, the deck angle now close to 45 degrees. Water was pouring into the bay with a terrifying, sucking roar. The lifeboats were already deployed or damaged. Their only option was the railing.

As they sprinted toward the rail, seeking the lowest point to jump, Mr. Harper's final backup—a fresh security team who had been waiting for the Rotterdam port arrival—emerged from a secured bulkhead door on the vehicle deck. They were the final, dedicated clean-up crew.

Arthur, covering his team's last steps, engaged them. He fired his sidearm until the slide locked open on empty. He reached for his final magazine, turning to fire again.

A sustained burst of fire slammed into his left thigh. The impact was sickening, bone-deep, and absolute. Arthur collapsed onto the slick, listing deck, the pistol skittering uselessly away. He was instantly disabled, his eyes wide with shock and the terror of leaving them exposed.

"Arthur!" Scarlett screamed, the terror overriding her exhaustion.

The role instantly reversed. Scarlett, ignoring the pain and the immediate threat, became the shield. She wrestled the GPMG from Rhys's hands.

"Go! Go! Go!" Scarlett roared, her voice raw with fury, unleashing a continuous, savage stream of fire from the GPMG, forcing the remaining mercenaries to take cover behind the commercial trucks and passenger vehicles filling the deck.

Ben and Rhys, ignoring their own wounds, dragged Arthur's heavy, inert body toward the railing. The deck was plunging into the freezing North Sea.

"Jump, Arthur! Jump, mate!" Ben yelled.

Rhys pushed Arthur over the railing just as the ship's lights flickered and died. Scarlett took one final look at the devastation, her face rigid with commitment. She dropped the heavy, smoking GPMG, and with a desperate final leap, plunged into the dark, icy depths after her husband. The roar of the sinking ship drowned out all sound.

Chapter 46: The North Sea Alibi

The impact with the water was a deep, shocking physical blow. Scarlett went under instantly, the freezing cold—the raw, absolute cold of the North Sea in November—a thousand needles piercing every inch of her exposed skin. Her lungs seized, locked tight against the icy shock, and the immense weight of her ruined wedding dress—the heavy satin, the dense layers of wet silk, the sodden corset bodice—acted like a lead anchor, dragging her down into the dark, churning depths.

Shock subsiding, Scarlett realized she was underwater, weighed down by the remnants of the vow she had just sealed. The dim pre-dawn light, filtered by the thick marine fog and the roiling water, created a terrifying twilight. She was surrounded by the debris field of the sinking ferry: shattered wood, life jackets, and the dark, inert shapes of the neutralized mercenaries. The chaos was silent, internal, and profound.

As she clawed her way up, kicking against the incredible drag of her dress and the heavy folds of fabric, she fought the physical urge to panic. Her training, the lessons Arthur had pounded into her about controlling her breath and conserving energy, were the only things overriding the instinct to thrash.

Her head finally broke through the surface, and she gasped a painful mouthful of frigid air. The waves were colossal, topped with foam and debris, the scent of diesel and brine overwhelming the clean air.

"ARTHUR!" she managed to shout, the sound thin and useless against the roar of the sea. "BEN!" "RHYS!" Nothing answered her but the sound of the waves slapping against the broken bits of the ferry's hull. She was alone, and cold, very cold. Her mind confirmed the devastating truth: the silk wedding dress provided no shield against November in the North Sea; it was now a shroud.

The Titanic Protocol

She quickly realized the terrifying reality: her sophisticated brain, the one that had hacked the Land Registry and defeated a criminal counsel, was useless against this environment. Her three months of specialized training had focused on *urban evasion and neutralization*, not *maritime survival*.

The only knowledge she could draw from was the absurd, profound memory of the film *Titanic*—a ridiculous piece of university trivia that suddenly seemed like gospel. *Find a door,* she thought, the mental instruction absurdly clear. *Find a door or something big enough to float.*

Swimming clumsily, hampered by the drag of the heavy, soaked silk, she maneuvered toward the nearest bit of large, black floating debris. It was a section of the bridge console—twisted steel and shattered glass—but it offered buoyancy. Hauling herself up onto the freezing, slick metal, she felt the raw agony of her bruised body and the crushing exhaustion of the swim.

She was now perched precariously on a metallic raft, exposed entirely to the elements. Her barrister's mind clicked back on, analyzing the variables. She calculated the rate of heat loss, the speed of the current, the minimal chance of immediate rescue. *We need a signal,* she determined. The boat sank with a tremendous explosion; surely someone saw it.

She pushed the ruined, heavy silk fabric of her skirt away from the metal, consciously exposing the vast expense of white silk still clinging to the bodice and the remnants of the train. It was a desperate gamble: her wedding dress, now a soaking white flag of surrender, was her final, visible signal against the dark sea and dense fog.

The Final Freeze

Arthur and his team were gone. She tried to pinpoint exactly when they were separated. The last memory was the sight of Rhys pushing Arthur over the railing. *They couldn't have been swept away that quickly. They must have drowned.* The despair was a cold weight in her chest.

The onset of hypothermia was slow, insidious, and terrifyingly gentle. The violent shivering eventually subsided, replaced by a deep, numbing cold that stole her awareness. Her mind grew slow, foggy. She realized her brain was shutting down, conserving energy, preparing for death.

I secured the vow, she thought distantly, the small victory irrelevant to the vast, crushing cold. *The marriage is legal. Logan is safe.* That single thought was the only thing holding the line against the soft oblivion. She knew she should paddle, should shout, should keep moving, but the freezing water made any further movement an impossible effort.

She was falling into a deep, final exhaustion when, through the dense marine fog, she heard it: the low, powerful engine noise of a search vessel.

The Unthinkable Cost

The sound grew loud, immediate, and utterly frantic. The small boat, the *Resolution*, appeared through the mist like a vengeful ghost, pitching violently on the swells. A figure, silhouetted against the dark deck, launched himself into the icy water. It was Ben.

He reached her quickly, his movements sharp and efficient. "Scarlett! Hold on!" he roared. He hooked a strong arm around her chest, ignoring her dead weight. He moved her toward the rescue vessel with brutal speed, pulling her through the chop.

She was hauled onto the deck by waiting hands, coughing and gagging on the brine. The deck was chaotic—ropes, medical supplies, and men moving with desperate speed. She was conscious just long enough to see the devastating tableau laid out on the cold metal deck.

Rhys was there, his face pale and drawn, applying relentless, forceful CPR to a heavy, unmoving form. The form was wearing dark, damaged tactical gear.

"Arthur," she whispered, the name a broken plea, the final realization of the cost hitting her. Before the overwhelming shock of the cold and the exhaustion consumed her entirely, the world went black.

Chapter 47: The Unseen Wounds

Arthur's eyes flickered open slightly. The first sound his mind registered was Rhys's voice, rough with immense exhaustion: "I've got him back."

He realized he was still swaying on the deck of a boat, the deck slippery with water tinged with blood. The vessel pitched violently against the heavy North Sea swell. Disorientation, sharp and immediate, seized him. He instinctively thought he was back in a combat zone, a worn-out forward operating base, surrounded by the familiar chaos of the forces. The pain was the only clarity.

A blinding, white-hot fire gripped his chest and torso. His hand instinctively snapped to his ribs. He groaned, the sound swallowed by the wind.

"Easy, buddy, we've got you," a voice, unfamiliar but authoritative, said. Arthur forced his eyes open, locating the speaker. It was a crew member from the *Resolution*, looking utterly terrified as he held a bag of clear fluid.

Clarity returned in agonizing pieces: the sinking ship, the final burst of fire, the terrible, sickening impact in his thigh. He looked down. Rhys, his face grim and utterly focused, was hunched over his leg, bathed in the harsh red light of the emergency lamp.

"What's the tally, Rhys?" Arthur managed to rasp, the words dry and weak.

"You took three rounds, you reckless bastard," Rhys replied, not looking up, his tone professional. "Two grazes to the shoulder and flank. The third, that one in your thigh, nicked the femoral artery and has splintered a chunk off your femur. I've got to get it out and close you up. Right now. I can give you pain relief—morphine—but I'm worried about it slowing your heart. We've only just got you back."

Arthur grit his teeth, feeling the pain of Rhys probing the wound with a sharp instrument—the agonizing precision required for field surgery near a major artery. "No," Arthur grunted, the pain driving the answer. "I'll survive. Do it."

Rhys went back to work, his movements precise and agonizingly slow. Arthur focused on the steel lines of the overhead gantry, breathing through the pain, using the internal discipline of his Special Reconnaissance training to block out the physical sensation. The agony was a cleansing fire, burning away the despair, leaving only pure, lethal intent.

The Last Word

He suddenly remembered the purpose of the fight. "Scarlett," Arthur rasped, attempting to sit up, but the move sent blinding spikes of pain through his ribs—he finally understood the sharp, newly acquired pain in his chest. "Where the fuck is Scarlett?"

Rhys immediately stopped his work, sliding up beside Arthur so they were face-to-face. He reached out and squeezed Arthur's uninjured shoulder.

"She's below deck, mate, in the medical hold," Rhys explained, his voice thick with the trauma of the retrieval. "Ben's with her. We're heading for the nearest military base—Dover—we've got a Medevac chopper waiting, but we're still hours out."

Arthur nodded, the news confirming his fear. "Her condition. Tell me."

Rhys sighed, the sound heavy. "She was in the water for about an hour before we found her. She was hypothermic, Arthur, dangerously cold. Ben had to cut that magnificent dress off before we could get the thermal blankets on. She was mumbling something about the *Titanic*. Mate, she nearly died."

Arthur absorbed the words, the image of Scarlett sinking in the freezing depths in her wedding dress—the gown that was meant to be their legal shield, turning into a lead weight—a fresh wave of terror. *She was actively swimming in the North Sea for an hour.* The sheer, stubborn, reckless determination was terrifying.

"And Logan?" Arthur demanded, the ultimate question.

"Logan is safe, Arthur. He's with Emily and Jade, secure at the cottage. We confirmed it five minutes ago. They're safe. We just need to get you two to a hospital before the bleed gets worse, and before your wife kills herself trying to heal you."

Rhys returned to the agonizing procedure, the sound of the metal instrument scraping near bone making Arthur groan despite his best efforts. The crew member, blessedly, was still holding the blood bag steady.

The Final Resolve

Arthur looked up at the ceiling of the small cabin, the light swaying with the choppy water. He was injured, immobilized, and separated from his son. He was going to spend weeks in recovery, relying on the system he fought to save.

"I have a Counterintelligence Counsel who fights with a pistol, a son in hiding, and a father-in-law holding an emergency custody order," he thought, focusing on the tactical summary of his life.

He focused on the single truth: Scarlett was alive. She was fighting. And she was giving them a chance to complete their lives. The cost was high, but the price of surrender was higher.

"Rhys," Arthur stated, his voice regaining its command despite the pain. "You seal that artery. You get me stable. We're going to use the next three months of recovery to plan Mr. Harper's final destruction. He hasn't won the war, mate. He's just given us a solid tactical injury leave."

The agony of the surgery intensified, but Arthur welcomed it. It was the price he paid for his family, and he would pay it all. They had to survive the sea before they could win the next war.

Chapter 48: The Warmth of Return

The first thing Scarlett registered was the profound, suffocating warmth. It was a clean, artificial warmth that felt like a thick plaster cast around her freezing body. She was lying down, the surface beneath her shifting gently with the swell of the sea. She was on a boat.

She opened her eyes, blinking against the low red light of a small cabin. She was wrapped entirely in a mound of rough, military-grade red blankets. A residual taste of brine and fuel oil clung to her mouth. She tried to move her arm and felt the dull ache of the old bullet wound and the new, searing agony across her entire body.

The man sitting patiently on a stool beside the bunk was Ben. He was meticulously cleaning his MP5, the focused, rhythmic action a familiar, stabilizing sight.

Ben looked up, his expression shifting instantly from operational vigilance to immense relief. "Hey, hey, Scarlett, you're awake."

Scarlett's mind raced, frantically piecing together the last memory: the GPMG, the plunge, the paralyzing cold, and the terrifying sight of Rhys applying CPR to Arthur.

"The water," she rasped, her voice thick and weak. "I'm naked?"

Ben paused, placing his weapon down and leaning toward her. "Yeah, I'm sorry about that, Scarlett. You were hypothermic. We had to get you out of that dress immediately. It was pure water weight, dragging you down." He said it matter-of-factly, the cold clinical truth overriding any awkwardness.

Oh great, she thought, the immediate humiliation replaced by profound gratitude for the medical necessity. *Arthur is going to love that debrief.*

"Wait, where's Arthur?" she demanded, attempting to sit up, instantly remembering the terrifying tableau. "Is he—"

"He's okay," Ben interrupted quickly, recognizing the panic. "He took three rounds. He's stable. He's in the med room right at the stern. He's sleeping, heavily medicated."

The Emergency Wardrobe

The relief was overwhelming, making her suddenly aware of her state. "Anyone got any clothes?" she asked, desperate for any armor against the reality.

Ben started laughing, a deep, weary sound. "We do, but you're not going to like it. It's the only thing that's sterile and warm on this boat." He pulled a thick, tightly wrapped bundle from a storage locker.

Scarlett forced herself to stand, her legs weak and unsteady. The clothes were indeed horrifying: a pair of brand new (thankfully) thermal long johns, military green, the thick material feeling like cardboard against her skin.

"They're designed for Arctic survival," Ben explained, suppressing a fresh laugh. "And they even have..."

Scarlett, realizing what was coming, sighed as she twisted around. "They even have an ass flap," she muttered, the grim absurdity of her current situation hitting her. She, the Counterintelligence Counsel, was standing naked in the middle of a warship, preparing to travel in a one-piece survival suit that exposed her backside with a buttoned hatch.

"The uniform of survival," Ben confirmed, helping her secure the last button.

The Cuddle Protocol

She moved through the narrow corridor toward the stern. Ben opened the door to the small, makeshift medical hold. Arthur lay on a railed hospital bed, pale and immense, his head lolling slightly with the steady, reassuring movement of the *Resolution*. His body was a map of bandages and IV ports.

She moved to the bedside, looking down at him. He seemed to sense her presence, his eyes fluttering open before fixing on her ridiculous, thermal-green silhouette.

He smiled faintly, a tired, genuine smile that vanished instantly as he took in her uniform. "What the fuck are you wearing?" he rasped, his voice rough with pain and surprise.

Scarlett laughed too, the sound tight, wincing instantly at the pain the movement caused his heavily medicated body. "The pinnacle of tactical fashion, darling. They called it 'Arctic Chic'."

"You okay? Do you need me to get Rhys?" Scarlett asked, seeing the genuine physical strain.

"No, my love," he said, his voice dropping to a soft, profound murmur, his eyes pulling her in. "I need my wife to get up on this bed with me and give me the biggest cuddle. I need to know you are real and warm."

She obliged instantly, crawling carefully next to his immense, still body, maneuvering around the IV lines and the heavily bandaged wounds. She tucked herself into his side, her rough, thermal uniform pressed against his hospital gown.

The soft hum of the *Resolution's* powerful engines deepened. They lay there, two damaged warriors, finally at rest, until the ship's horn bellowed, signaling their arrival.

"We're here," Arthur whispered. The Medevac team would be waiting at the dock in Dover, ready to whisk them both to a secure UK military hospital. The physical escape was over; the healing could finally begin.

Chapter 49: The Unacceptable Oversight

The small cottage kitchen was bathed in the soft, twinkling light of the Christmas tree. It was 10:00 AM on Christmas Eve. Outside, the moor was grey and quiet. Arthur stared at the blinking lights, profoundly miserable. He was stuck on mandated bed rest—battered, bandaged, and effectively neutralized.

Every morning, since they'd been home, Scarlett would get up with Logan, bring him into Arthur for a quick cuddle, make breakfast (which they'd eat together in bed), and then get Logan ready for the secure Met crèche and herself ready for the Manchester office. She always left him his pad and the TV remote, the new mini-fridge Ben had brought full of healthy snacks and drinks. But the moment she was gone, the idleness became torture.

He'd hobbled downstairs, logged into the secure terminal, and started watching her at the office. It started because he missed her, but after two months, it had metastasized into absolute, operational paranoia. He'd watched her for nearly two months.

The Live Assault

Turning his attention back to the office surveillance feed, Arthur watched the corridor camera. He spotted her weaving her way down the corridor, a pile of folders in her uninjured right arm. She was dressed in his favorite skirt, a tight A-line that hugged her shape perfectly, and a matching fitted jacket.

The scene escalated instantly. Scarlett was bent over the console in the office, the pile of files next to the screen, clearly engrossed in what she was doing and didn't notice that prick enter.

Arthur watched the camera switch to the internal office view. Dickson leant over Scarlett, ostensibly to look at the console. Arthur felt his blood pressure spike. "He's in the room with her," Arthur grated, his fury low and dangerous.

Then, Dickson deliberately placed his hands on her hips, pulling her toward him.

Scarlett shot upright, instantly pulling away from the unwanted touch. Her hands went up in a clear, universal demand for space. "Get your hands off me, Dickson! That's unprofessional!"

Dickson ignored her. He grabbed her by the hips and pulled her hard into him, pinning her against the terminal.

Arthur was screaming silent instructions at the screen, consuming with helpless rage. He could see Rhys break into a run down the corridor on the external feed.

In the office feed, Rhys burst through the door. "Harper! I need that Ogben file reference now!" Rhys demanded, diverting Dickson.

The distraction was the only chance Scarlett needed. She used the second of surprise to deliver a savage, precise sucker punch to Dickson's face. Dickson staggered back, disoriented by the force, but immediately went to lunge at her. Rhys, already moving, grabbed Dickson and slammed him against the wall, neutralizing him instantly.

The Unacceptable Oversight (Conclusion)

Rhys then went back to Scarlett, grabbing her, pulling her close as she started to shake and sob, the adrenaline and shock finally breaking her composure.

Rhys looked directly into the camera on the secure terminal, still hugging Scarlett but giving Arthur a sharp thumbs up.

Arthur sat back, the breath rushing out of his lungs. He wanted to call her, to hear her voice, but he couldn't. He knew the risk. He sat there, staring at the screen, the only sound the faint, joyful ringing of jingle bells playing on the radio, profoundly grateful for the Met's clean crew. The siege was ongoing, even on Christmas Eve.

Chapter 50: Sanctuary and Baileys

The cold tile of the secure office bathroom floor felt sharp beneath Scarlett's shoes. Her hands were shaking violently, not from the physical contact—the punch she landed on Dickson's jaw had been clean and gratifying—but from the violent surge of PTSD that followed. She knew she was close to sobbing, but she held the tears back until Rhys had neutralized the situation.

Rhys had left, having been placated by Scarlett's insistence that the immediate threat was contained, but the psychological damage was done. The sudden, unwanted grab at her hips had instantly transported her back to the concrete cell in Manchester, back into Michael's hands, reliving the degradation. She worked until 5:00 PM, running the final files, using the routine and the cold professionalism of her task to steady herself.

The drive home was a forced pep talk, determined not to let her raw emotional state alert Arthur's sharp suspicion. She pulled into the drive, the sight of the small cottage—their precarious sanctuary—a profound relief.

Arriving home, she found Arthur already out of bed, violating his doctor's orders. He was propped up on the sofa. "You're supposed to be in bed," she sighed, handing a squirming Logan—who was shouting a loud, insistent "Daddy!"—to him. The sight of Arthur's immense frame struggling to contain their one-year-old son brought a genuine smile to her face.

"It's Christmas Eve," Arthur replied, pulling Logan close. "I thought we could do something Christmassy."

She looked at him skeptically. "Mr. Grinch wants to do something Christmassy?"

He nodded, his eyes soft. "I watched the movie, didn't I? I'm integrating. I thought we could decorate the mantle and finally watch *A Muppet Christmas Carol*."

"That would be lovely," she agreed, her heart soaring at the unexpected domesticity. "Let me grab a shower and I'm all yours. Oh, and don't let me forget to put the turkey in to cook before we go to bed."

"That turkey's big enough to sustain us until February," Arthur joked, his smile genuine.

The Cleansing Ritual

Scarlett left them, carrying the heavy weight of the day's events into the bathroom. She ripped her clothes off as quickly as possible, dropping the professional garments onto the floor. *He touched them,* she said to herself, the contact—the violation of her personal space—had left a residue worse than physical pain.

As soon as the hot water hit her, the tears fell. She just stood there sobbing, letting the shame and the rage wash out, cleansing the memory of Dickson's unwanted hands. The weeping was deep, exhausting, but necessary. Once purged, she dried herself with care, lingering over the scars on her body—the map of their shared trauma.

She emerged, dressed in soft, clean loungewear, the emotional purge complete. She and Arthur spent the evening in a carefully constructed bubble of normalcy. They decorated the sparse mantle with pine cones, ate a simple, comforting meal, and cuddled on the sofa, opening small, early gifts. Arthur, surprisingly, produced his heavy recon camera (stupidly HD) and took a beautiful family selfie—the three of them, warm and safe, their faces scarred but finally laughing.

Later, she laid out the matching sets of Christmas pajamas she had bought for them all. PJs in the day was alien to Arthur's disciplined background, but he surprised her by putting them on immediately, admitting, "It's a tradition I'm going to learn to love."

Scarlett knew the domestic facade was their shield.

She helped Arthur upstairs, mindful of his still-recovering injuries, before slipping downstairs to put the turkey in (Arthur had genuinely forgotten, despite his excellent memory) and lock the cottage doors.

The Quiet Vow

They settled in bed, the lights low. She pulled the bottle of Baileys from her bag.

"Fancy drinking this in bed?" she said to him, expecting him to refuse due to his meds or discourage her because of his condition.

"I'd love to," he surprised her.

They shared the bottle, the sweetness and warmth fighting the emotional cold, chatting about random rubbish—Logan's new words, Rhys's terrible suit, the bizarre logistics of coordinating Christmas dinner from a secure bunker. They got tipsier, the alcohol dulling the edges of their exhaustion. Arthur didn't initiate intimacy; he chose only to love on her and kiss her with quiet devotion. He was focused on intimacy and security, not performance.

Scarlett was grateful for the pause. She pulled herself up onto her elbow, her smile wide and wicked, fueled by the Baileys and the certainty of their future. She kissed him deeply, lingeringly, before whispering, "I have one final surprise for you under the bed, Detective. But it's for tomorrow night. After Logan is asleep."

Arthur's eyes softened completely, acknowledging the commitment and the enforced delay. He pulled her close, his good arm wrapping gently around her. They fell asleep tangled together, cuddling, the ghosts of the past silenced, if only for Christmas morning.

Chapter 51: The Cost of Isolation

The quiet darkness of the cottage bedroom was absolute. Arthur was the first awake, the dull, aching pain in his surgical sites rousing him well before dawn. He lay still for a moment, listening to the deep, steady breathing of Scarlett beside him.

He fumbled around the nightstand with his good arm, finding the bottle of water and the required morning pain medication. The rattling of the plastic disturbed Scarlett.

"You okay, gorgeous?" she asked sleepily, her voice soft and rough with sleep.

Momentarily shocked by the unexpected term of endearment, Arthur paused. "Yes, beautiful. Just need drugs and a piss."

Scarlett's eyes opened properly, and she registered his struggle to sit up, his movements stiff and limited by the healing grazes on his flank and the metal pins in his leg. Despite Arthur's immediate protests, she got up, ignoring her own exhaustion. She stood next to him, effortlessly popping out his morning meds and handing him the water bottle from the floor.

"Can you handle the piss yourself?" she teased, her voice regaining its playful strength. "Or am I okay to check the turkey?"

Arthur managed a pained laugh and let her help him out of the bed, the physical support a profound act of trust. By the time he'd managed to shuffle back to bed, completing the necessary morning rituals, she was already back in it and blessedly unconscious, pulled back down by the deep sleep her body desperately needed.

He decided that he was awake and would leave her to sleep. The house was quiet, and the sun was yet to rise. He had a few surprises he wanted to get out ready.

The Secret Vice: Amazon Logistics

Secret spying hadn't been his only vice whilst on mandated bed rest. He had discovered Amazon. Confined and immobilized, Arthur had leveraged the secure, untraceable banking systems of the Met to wage a furious, emotional campaign against the commercial giant. Every purchase was routed through different decoy addresses and delivered to a safe drop point—a logistical nightmare of covert parenting.

Already in his matching Christmas PJs—a concession to her obsession he now secretly enjoyed—he made his way carefully down the stairs. The house was cold, but the scent of pine and woodsmoke was strong. He pulled several heavy storage bags of presents from the shed outside, dragging them inside the warm cottage and stacking them neatly beneath the tree.

His selection was meticulous, fueled by the terrifying realization of how close he had come to losing his future.

He had bought everything Scarlett loved: a rare, vintage band T-shirt from a defunct pop-punk band; a massive, expensive bottle of Jack Daniel's (a silent, loving acknowledgment of her need for release and a promise of safe space); and a stunning piece of jewelry—not the river stone, but a new white gold band set with lab-grown diamonds. He had specifically chosen lab-grown because he knew her ethical stance on natural diamonds and the brutal conflict associated with them.

For Logan, the gifts were pure Arthur: a V-Tech DJ deck (a nod to his former cover) and a stack of miniature clothes that made him look suspiciously like a toddler in fatigues—a controlled, silent joke.

The Unpacking of Love

He was positioning the last gift when the kitchen floorboards creaked. Scarlett was standing there, wrapped in her festive pajamas, carrying a demanding Logan on her hip.

"Well, look who decided to join the civilian ranks," Scarlett teased, her eyes soft.

Arthur was already at the stove, his focus on the iron skillet. He had planned the morning meticulously. "I thought a full English was necessary before the present destruction began."

The next few hours were spent in a blur of domestic chaos. They ate breakfast together—a glorious, over-the-top fry-up—and then settled by the fire to open gifts. Arthur watched, captivated, as Logan, enthralled by the wrapping paper, conducted the session.

Scarlett's reaction to his gifts was profound. She laughed at the JD, kissed him fiercely for the band T-shirt, and finally gasped when she opened the ring box.

"Arthur," she whispered, tears in her eyes, "the lab-grown diamonds... you remembered."

"I remember everything, my love," he murmured, his thumb tracing the new, brilliant band he placed beside the river stone.

Arthur, in turn, was choked up by his own presents. Scarlett had spoiled him: high-end tactical boots (not traceable to any Met supplier), a massive new supply of obscure coffee beans, and a first-edition signed copy of a military history book he'd casually mentioned months ago. He realized with devastating clarity that she knew him so well—his need for security, his intellectual pursuits, and his quiet devotion.

The afternoon was spent cooking a sprawling Christmas dinner together, managing the domestic coordination (Scarlett directing Arthur, Logan napping) that was far more complex than any Met extraction plan. They ate the meal together, enjoying the simple, hard-won peace before settling in front of the TV for Christmas specials.

The Final Vow

As evening settled, Scarlett carried the now-quieted Logan upstairs and settled him into his cot. He paused, watching the rhythmic rise and fall of his son's chest, ensuring the security protocol was engaged.

He shuffled back to the bedroom. Scarlett was already there, pulling herself up onto her elbow, her eyes bright and fueled by the day's love and the lingering sweetness of the Baileys.

"Now, its time for your special present," Scarlett purred sultrily, her voice thick with promise. She reached under the bed and retrieved a small, wrapped box. "Lock the door, Detective."

Arthur's heart hammered a frantic rhythm. He secured the door and moved as fast as his bandaged body allowed, shedding his pajama top as he went.

He found her laid in a sexy pose, wearing the lingerie he'd only ever seen in lad mags: bright red bra and knickers with a festive fluffy white trim. "Fucking hell, you look... wow," he managed, his exhaustion dissolving entirely.

She rushed forward, pulling his remaining PJs down and helping him into the bed. She didn't wait. She immediately mounted him, straddling his waist, sliding herself onto his hardness.

"What did I do to deserve this?" he managed to say, his voice thick with raw passion.

"Well, this," she purred, indicating the new wedding ring on her finger, "bought a LOT of brownie points." She started riding him, slowly at first, leaning down to bite his neck.

Arthur's hands cupped her hips, rising to meet her rhythm, his focus now solely on the feeling of their complete connection. He moved his hands deliberately, running his palm over the smooth skin of her abdomen, briefly tracing the scar on her flank, a visible tribute to their survival. He lowered her bra with his good hand. They reached their climax together, falling onto each other, the quiet, profound love of their hard-won life sealing the final vow.

Chapter 52: The Operational Hand-off

The quiet cottage, still faintly perfumed by the pine and woodsmoke of Christmas past, felt less like a sanctuary and more like a high-security holding cell. Arthur Jacobs, confined to the kitchen counter by his surgical sites, pushed a half-empty mug of cooling tea away. He was a creature of perpetual motion, and his current state was a professional death.

His internal frustration was palpable, rooted in the final diagnosis delivered remotely an hour ago: six months of mandated bed rest. The timeline stretched ahead of him—six months of staring at walls, six months of relying on Amazon logistics—six months of being functionally irrelevant.

The scent of woodsmoke shifted as the outer door clicked open. Deedee Hayes, his Detective Inspector, walked in, her crisp uniform and sharp focus an immediate collision with the cottage's lingering domesticity. She bypassed the remnants of the holiday, going straight to the core issue.

"Status report, Jacobs," she clipped, placing a secure tablet on the table.

"Medicated, immobile, and functionally redundant," Arthur grated, the assessment brutal because it was true. "The Ledger is secure. What's the loss ratio from the courtroom attack?"

"The Ledger is secure. Mr. Harper is in custody, but his legal shield is impenetrable—he's delaying the Tainted Evidence hearing indefinitely," Deedee confirmed, pulling up a map. "Gary and the Mole escaped, confirmed on CCTV at Heathrow this morning. They're liquidating assets in Europe."

Arthur's eyes narrowed, ignoring the pain in his leg. "And my operational future?"

"The six months is non-negotiable. Medical mandate," Deedee repeated, delivering the final blow. "But you're still active. Your role is Remote Tactical Lead. Comms support only."

She pulled up the map of Prague's financial district. "We are assigning the operational lead to the one asset the OCG has consistently underestimated."

Arthur felt the familiar spike of cold dread, the professional certainty colliding with the personal terror. "No. Deedee. Her recovery—"

Deedee cut him off, her voice snapping with command. "Arthur, stop. She has full operational clearance. She is the LFO. She has the capability to navigate Radek's financial firewalls and the legal cover to get boots on the ground without triggering an international incident."

She spoke the words that were Arthur's new prison: "Scarlett is now the Lead Field Operative (LFO), reporting directly to me. Your primary function is to keep her alive."

Arthur's jaw clenched, the anger and the pride warring beneath his skin. This wasn't professional ascent; this was forced sacrifice. His paralysis was her exposure.

He forced the fury down, pushing it into a cold, diamond-hard shell of operational focus. "She is not to engage with Radek directly. Digital extraction only. Her security perimeter must be tripled. I want the feed routed directly to this house, twenty-four seven. I want full telemetry on her vitals and location. If that perimeter is compromised, I authorize immediate Met team insertion, regardless of jurisdiction."

"Agreed," Deedee said, relief evident that he hadn't fully broken. "She leaves for the Prague staging area at 0400 hours tomorrow."

Arthur looked toward the stairs, where Scarlett still slept, unaware of the operational hand-off. His operational mind knew the logic was lethal, perfect, and necessary. But the husband was terrified.

Chapter 53: The Cost of Command

Scarlett stood in the quiet kitchen, the cold scent of post-Christmas woodsmoke clinging to the air, watching Deedee Hayes leave. The door clicked shut with a brutal finality that sealed her new operational mandate. She was the Lead Field Operative (LFO); she was going to Prague.

She turned slowly, taking in the scene. Arthur was still leaning heavily against the counter, his face a mask of furious, concentrated defeat. His operational mind had seized command, issuing the directives that would govern her mission, but his body—the source of his power and her security—was a broken liability.

"Prague," Scarlett repeated, her voice steady, professional, masking the sharp, cold spike of terror that had just lodged beneath her ribs. "Four thousand hours. Digital extraction only."

She walked towards Arthur, placing her hand gently on his uninjured shoulder, feeling the taut, rigid muscle beneath the cotton of his Christmas PJs.

"Arthur," she murmured, "Look at me. This is not your fault."

His dark eyes, usually so sharp and commanding, were clouded with self-recrimination and fear. "It is entirely my fault, Scarlett," he grated, the pain in his leg and shoulder making his voice tight. "I made the move. I broke the protocol. I let Gary win the custody battle in the courtroom, and now I have to watch you clean up the mess from a bloody remote feed."

Scarlett leaned into him. "This is Deedee's call, not mine," she whispered, a necessary lie to ease his fury. "And I am qualified. You trained me for this, Arthur. Every brutal, necessary, ridiculous minute of it."

The memory of the last two months of training—the relentless conditioning that replaced her solicitor polish with steel—was their devastating joint legacy. He had forged her into this weapon, and now the Met was deploying her.

She pulled back, forcing lightness into her tone. "We have ten hours until deployment. You need a proper debrief, not just a map point. You need to tell me everything Radek is hiding, everything you suspect about the mole's comms method, and you need a new painkiller regimen that doesn't rely on me guessing the dose."

Arthur swallowed hard, the shift in focus—from emotional crisis to operational necessity—his only escape route. He nodded stiffly. "We start with the Radek file. I need to brief you on the comms bypass protocols. There are things Deedee won't put on the tablet."

They moved with the strained, practiced rhythm of a long-married couple preparing for war. Scarlett secured the cottage, checking the battery levels on the two secure laptops and setting up the advanced encryption keys. She boiled the kettle, made strong tea—lots of milk, the way she liked it—and gently guided Arthur to the sofa, propping his leg up with pillows.

But the domestic peace was a facade. Every click of the laptop key, every whisper of technical jargon, was a screaming reminder of the life they were fighting to maintain.

Later, huddled under the blanket on the sofa, with the operational maps spread across the coffee table, Scarlett paused. She looked at the presents still stacked beneath the pine tree, relics of their brief, beautiful holiday. She realized the enormity of what they were doing. They were prioritizing the Ledger, the professional cleanup, over the very real danger that Logan, now under the rotating care of trusted (but still exposed) Met personnel, was vulnerable. The threat was still alive. Her father was still launching legal attacks, and the one person she trusted implicitly to be the unmoving foundation of their safety was now the fragile one.

"Arthur," she whispered, setting the file down. "Logan. He's safe?"

The question was the break in the dam. Arthur's composure fractured. "He's secure, Scarlett. Jade is running the rotation, and she's clean. But I should be there. I should be the one checking the perimeter. Not here, telling my wife how to breach a network that was designed by a psychopath."

He reached out, his hand gripping her wrist, the urgency intense. "You promised me no more field work, Scarlett. You promised me stability."

"And you promised me the bassline would be silenced," she countered softly, her gaze unwavering. "We are finishing this, Arthur. Together. I go to Prague,

I retrieve the final ledger, and we come home. And then, you teach me how to stop using the comms feed to order Amazon for an entire year. Deal?"

The trade-off was brutal, laced with fierce love and necessary sacrifice. Arthur knew he had no choice. He could fight Deedee, he could fight the Met, but he couldn't fight the unassailable logic of his wife's determination, which mirrored his own.

He pulled her closer, his lips finding hers in a kiss that was a desperate, fierce vow—not to stability, but to survival. He was tethered; she was deployed. The remote feed was their only lifeline, and their operational marriage, built on chaos and trust, was the only thing standing between them and permanent ruin.

Chapter 54: The View from the Cage

The clock on the secure laptop screen read 03:58. Arthur didn't need the visual confirmation; the stillness in the cottage was loud enough to announce the approaching deadline. He was propped up on the sofa, his fractured leg elevated on a mound of pillows, the medical brace a rigid, unforgiving shell against his skin. The Christmas PJs felt less like domestic comfort and more like a costume of failure.

He was the Remote Tactical Lead.

Across the room, bathed in the cool glow of the computer monitor, Scarlett moved with a quiet, lethal efficiency that both paralyzed and terrified him. She wasn't wearing silk or sparkly rave tops; she was clad in dark, functional, Met-issued field gear—a practical uniform that screamed competence and imminent danger. She was checking the satellite battery packs, adjusting the earpiece of her comms rig, the cold discipline of the operative entirely overriding the warm softness of his wife.

Arthur watched her, his professional pride battling a primal, visceral scream of sheer helplessness. He had trained her for this. Every brutal, necessary drill, every harsh word, every sleepless night spent preparing her for the inevitable. But he had prepared her to be *his* asset, under *his* command, where he could take the bullet. He hadn't prepared her to be deployed by a cold, faceless institution while he was condemned to watch from a surveillance feed.

"Comms check," Arthur grated, his voice tight from disuse and tension.

Scarlett pressed the comms button near her throat. "Check. Clear. Encryption holding on the primary channel."

"Radek's known routines," Arthur continued, forcing his voice into the flat, professional rhythm of command he knew she needed. "He arrives at 07:00, leaves at 19:00. The digital ledger is backed up at midnight local. You are in-and-out before 06:00. If the backup fails, you abort. Do you understand, Scarlett? No contingency, no compromise."

"Understood. Digital extraction only," she affirmed, not looking at him, her focus entirely externalized. "Minimum exposure."

The terms of the engagement were excruciatingly specific, designed to minimize the possibility of the close-quarters combat he knew she was more than capable of. He saw her secure the lock-picking kit in a hidden compartment of her utility vest, her movements fluid, practiced, and entirely independent.

03:59.

Arthur reached for the mouse, bringing up the live feeds on the secondary laptop. Rhys and Ben, his most trusted operational assets, were already positioned in the unmarked vehicle near the cottage gate. They would form her immediate perimeter, but the comms link to them felt brittle, remote. He was relying on their loyalty, on their training, and on the unassailable faith that they would protect her better than he currently could.

Scarlett walked over to the sofa. She didn't offer a hug—the professional discipline was too high for that—but she knelt beside him, placing a hand gently over his braced leg.

"I need you to stay off the comms unless I call or unless you see a red flag on the feed," she instructed, her voice soft but absolute. "Your panic is a liability. Your job is to be my stability. Don't be a source of chaos, Arthur."

The quiet authority in her voice—the voice of a field commander establishing the rules of engagement with her Comms support—was a devastating reversal of their dynamic. He realized, with a sickening clarity, that she was entirely ready for this.

"I'll be here," Arthur managed, his throat thick. "Watching everything. Every single second."

She squeezed his leg, a silent acknowledgment of the brutal trade-off they were making. "I love you. I'm coming home."

Then, she was gone.

The silence that descended on the cottage was absolute. Arthur heard the quiet click of the front door, the crunch of her boots on the frozen ground outside, then the low, muffled sound of the unmarked engine pulling away.

He pushed the pillows away, ignoring the searing pain in his thigh, forcing himself into a semi-upright position. He lunged for the laptop, bringing the operational feeds into full-screen focus.

The screen provided the only reality now: a grainy thermal image showing three distinct figures moving through the darkness toward the extraction vehicle. Her bio-telemetry feed blinked steadily in the corner: heart rate 75 bpm. Calm. Too calm.

He reached for the mug of tea she had made for him, but the liquid was cold. The adrenaline that should have been coursing through his veins was trapped in his body, paralyzed by the brace. It was all flowing into the digital cable connecting him to the outside world.

He was the ghost, condemned to watch her walk into the fire he couldn't reach. The true horror of his six-month sentence had begun. He was useless—a tactical map reader, a voice in a remote earpiece, a terrified husband trapped behind glass, watching his wife command the war he was supposed to be fighting.

He watched the little green icon representing her position move slowly away from the perimeter, merging with the larger dots of Rhys and Ben. He knew the risks: Radek, the Mole, institutional betrayal, and the sheer, unpredictable chaos of a city determined to fight back.

Arthur leaned his head back against the sofa, his eyes burning into the screen, prepared for the longest, most agonizing night of his life.

Chapter 55: The Black Ops Tourist

Scarlett felt the familiar, low vibration of the unmarked vehicle beneath her feet, a subtle hum that always settled her nerves. Beside her, Rhys was a silent, professional anchor, his eyes scanning the urban landscape of the Prague staging area. She had officially crossed the line. She was the Lead Field Operative (LFO); the Ledger's fate, and Arthur's, rested on her success.

The adrenaline, which had been trapped by the pre-deployment tension, now coursed through her, sharp and clarifying. Yet, beneath the professional veneer, the raw, personal ache of the separation was immense. She knew Arthur was now pinned to the comms link in the cottage, his professional expertise serving as her tether, his mind a battlefield of terror and control.

Don't be a source of chaos, she could hear her own voice echoing the operational instruction she had given him. The irony was a bitter taste—she, the chaotic lawyer, was demanding stability from the man forged in control.

She pressed the comms button near her throat. "Status check, Comms Lead. Sound clear?"

Arthur's voice was instantaneous in her earpiece, tight and strained, yet disciplined. "Affirmative, LFO. Sound clear. Heart rate stable, but climbing. Just focus on the parameters, Scarlett."

She mentally corrected him: *LFO*. Not Scarlett. That compartmentalization was the only way they would both survive the next ten hours.

"Understood, Comms Lead," she confirmed, pulling the urban map of Prague onto her secure tablet. "Rhys, we dismount four blocks from the target bank. Ben secures the final perimeter. I go in under the tourist pre-text."

Her cover was ridiculously simple: an exhausted, slightly lost British lawyer who needed emergency document retrieval before a critical international court filing. Her field gear, stripped of heavy armor and external weapons, was minimalist: the specialized lock-picking kit, the digital extraction hardware, and her legal tablet. Her primary weapon was not the sidearm Arthur had secured for the perimeter team, but the flawless, high-speed coding and legal jargon he had trained her to deploy.

The vehicle slowed, pulling into a concealed spot behind a historic square. The city felt alive, bustling with the false normalcy of early morning activity that was perfect for camouflage.

"Dismount," Arthur instructed, his voice now purely tactical. "Comms check every ten minutes. No exceptions. Ben is running thermal surveillance on the building entrance."

Scarlett nodded to Rhys, the signal silent. She moved, leaving the security of the vehicle and plunging into the foreign crowd. She adopted the Black Ops Tourist posture immediately: eyes darting (but focused on target recognition), body language slightly hurried (but intentional), wearing clothes that were expensive enough to denote importance but bland enough to denote anonymity.

The target, Radek's private asset management bank, was a baroque monstrosity of carved stone and brass, the perfect architectural disguise for high-level financial crime.

As she moved across the square, a sudden, familiar wave of nausea hit her, a cold spike of panic that had nothing to do with Radek or the Mole. She pressed the comms button immediately, pushing the panic down.

"Comms Lead, I have multiple thermal signatures on the secondary rooftops. Confirming Met assets or external threat," she clipped, forcing her voice level.

"Negative, LFO," Arthur replied instantly. "Rhys confirms standard commercial roofing access. Heart rate is spiking. What is your true status, Scarlett?"

She hated that he could read her so easily through the technology, that the digital cable connecting them was also a direct feed into her central nervous system.

"Current status: stable, Comms Lead. Just a sudden surge of adrenaline," she lied, navigating past a busy café terrace. The truth was far more domestic: the exhaustion from the last two months, the abrupt change in her diet, and the gnawing anxiety over Logan. The personal vulnerability threatened to overwhelm the professional discipline she was desperately trying to maintain.

She reached the alley leading to the bank's service entrance, the air cooler and smelling faintly of diesel and decay.

"Ben is in position," Arthur announced. "The target is locked. LFO, you are cleared to proceed with digital extraction. Remember the protocol: in-and-out before 06:00. If the backup fails, you abort."

"Understood, Comms Lead," she whispered. She paused, adjusting the earpiece. "Arthur?"

She heard the sharp intake of his breath in her ear—the sound of the husband momentarily overriding the handler. "What is it, Scarlett?"

"I just needed to hear your voice."

A long second of silence stretched across the satellite feed, heavy with their shared emotional chaos.

"Go, LFO," Arthur finally grated, the sound thick with pain and love. "Be brilliant."

Scarlett took a deep breath, the cold air filling her lungs. She moved toward the reinforced service door, the lock-picking kit ready in her hand. The fate of their future—her legal defense, Arthur's career, and Logan's safety—was not in the Ledger, but in the speed of her fingers and the clarity of her focus. She was in command, and the mission had begun.

Chapter 56: The Digital Dread

The clock on the secure laptop screen was now meaningless. For Arthur, the world had shrunk to the four corners of the high-resolution monitor displaying the Radek financial bank in Prague. The time read 05:15, local Prague time. Scarlett had been inside the facility for fifty-two minutes.

Arthur lay on the sofa, bathed in the cool, blue-white light of the screen, his entire body a rigid map of silent agony. The pain from his fractured femur and pinned shoulder was a dull, constant roar, but the real torment was the digital silence. Every second stretched, amplified, carrying the crushing weight of his operational redundancy.

He was the Comms Lead, but he was useless.

The screen provided two lines of defense and one line of offense. The defense was the thermal feed: Rhys and Ben, two distinct thermal signatures positioned discreetly across the square, silently protecting the perimeter. The offense was the digital meter on the corner of the screen, indicating Scarlett's signal stability and the agonizingly slow progress of the digital extraction she was running via a secure injection point.

Progress: 42%.

Comms Status: Silent.

Heart Rate: 98 bpm.

Arthur pushed the comms button. "Comms check, LFO. Report status. You are thirty minutes past estimated ingress time."

"Comms Lead," Scarlett's voice was instantaneous in his earpiece, tight and clipped. "Ingress time compromised by updated security protocol. Manual override required. Extraction stability confirmed. Progress holding. I'm inside the central firewall. Working."

Her voice was all he had. It was the only barrier between his terror and the chaos she was navigating. He could hear the faint, distant clicking of her keyboard through the satellite feed—the sound of his wife battling Radek's financial firewalls in the heart of Europe.

"Acknowledge, LFO. Maintain silence unless the feed drops or the backup fails. Your heart rate is fluctuating. You are pushing too hard, Scarlett."

"Acknowledge, Comms Lead. Your panic is noted," she clipped back, the field operative correcting the stability of the handler.

Arthur swallowed the professional reprimand, the sheer audacity of her operational confidence battling his personal dread. He pulled up the thermal feed, focusing on the exterior. The streets were starting to wake. The civilian traffic was increasing—the perfect camouflage for her extraction, but also for an enemy insertion.

He focused on the progress meter. 48%.

He realized with a cold clarity that this prolonged digital silence was far worse than the noisy chaos of a direct firefight. In a fight, he would know the vector, the enemy, the immediate threat. In this silence, the enemy was invisible, digital, and could be anywhere. The Mole, Gary—they could be watching this exact connection, waiting for her to surface.

Arthur reached for the cold tea she had made him, ignoring the stiffness in his surgical sites. He desperately missed the brutal clarity of physical action—the ability to move, to strike, to protect. He was trained to be the kinetic shield, and his helplessness felt like a tactical failure.

Progress: 55%.

He saw a thermal anomaly on the rooftop across from the bank—a quick flash of heat, then silence. He immediately zoomed the feed.

"Comms Lead to Ben, report roofline visual on the adjacent building. Confirm clear."

"Comms Lead, this is Ben. Roof clear. Commercial exhaust fan signature only. Visual confirmed."

Arthur leaned back, letting out a breath he didn't realize he'd been holding. He was overcompensating, running every scenario in his head, turning mundane commercial activity into existential threat. He was letting his personal fear compromise his operational command. He was the chaos she had warned him against.

Don't be a source of chaos.

He closed his eyes, forcing himself to relax his grip on the mouse. He focused on her heartbeat: a steady, high-pitched thump-thump in the digital feed, the only rhythmic reality in the surreal world of electronic warfare.

05:45.

"Comms Lead to LFO," Arthur whispered, keeping his voice low, steady, and devoid of personal panic. "Report progress. Abort window is closing."

"Comms Lead, extraction is at 98%. File transfer stability confirmed. Retrieving final registry keys now."

A jolt of sharp, intense relief shot through Arthur's body, overriding the pain. He saw the meter jump: 100%.

"Extraction confirmed. LFO, commence immediate exfil. Move! Move! Move!"

He watched the screen, terrified. Her heart rate spiked immediately: 130 bpm. He saw her thermal signature move quickly away from the injection point. He had the Ledger. Now he just needed his wife.

Chapter 57: The Ghost in the Baroque

The sharp, sudden urgency in Arthur's voice—"Extraction confirmed. LFO, commence immediate exfil. Move! Move! Move!"—was the only permission Scarlett needed. The digital file transfer, a slow, agonizing drain of her focus, was complete. The Ledger was theirs.

The relative silence of the bank vault's server room shattered as she moved. Her heart rate, which had climbed steadily during the digital infiltration, spiked further, hitting 130 bpm. The transition from intellectual warfare to physical action was jarring, yet exhilarating. She disconnected the digital injection point, securing the specialized hardware back into the hidden compartment of her vest.

In and out before 06:00.

The mantra was her only guide. She retracted the lock-picking tension wrench from the exterior panel with a practiced, silent click. She moved, becoming the Black Ops Tourist again, moving with a controlled, hurried gait through the pristine, marble-lined hallway.

"Comms Lead, LFO is moving toward the service exit. ETA to dismount point: five minutes," she whispered into the comms mic, her breath ragged.

"Acknowledge, LFO. Ben reports an anomaly," Arthur's voice was sharp, immediate, stripped of any pretense of comfort. "A private vehicle, unregistered, has pulled into the alley adjacent to your exfil point. It is stationary. Confirming enemy insertion or observation."

The news was a sickening internal blow. They were compromised. The Mole was working faster than expected, or Gary had a contingency in place.

Scarlett immediately pivoted, abandoning the direct route. She plunged into the employee stairwell—a concrete, claustrophobic space that smelled faintly of old coffee and bleach. The acoustic difference was instantaneous; the silence was thick, amplifying the sound of her operational boots against the steel treads.

"Comms Lead, overriding primary exfil. Diverting to rooftop access via maintenance ladder. Advising Rhys to redeploy to the adjacent rooftop for extraction cover," she commanded, the adrenaline honing her tactical focus.

"Negative, LFO! That violates the exposure parameter! Get to the ground, Scarlett!" Arthur's voice was raw—the sound of the husband momentarily overriding the Comms Lead.

"I don't have time for the ground, Comms Lead. Trust the training," she snapped back, climbing two steps at a time. The sheer physical exertion was a welcome distraction from the mounting fear over the stationary vehicle.

She emerged onto the roof access door, kicking the emergency bar with a focused burst of energy. The air hit her face—cold, damp, and smelling of diesel and old stone. She was surrounded by the grotesque splendor of Prague's baroque skyline.

She ran, navigating the maze of air conditioning units and satellite dishes toward the adjacent building, which housed the pre-planned exfil vehicle.

"I see her," Rhys's voice cut in, bypassing Arthur's channel. "Moving to intercept point. Arthur, we've got company on the street—two men dismounting from the vehicle, moving toward the bank entrance."

"Negative! They are moving to intercept *her*!" Arthur screamed, his voice strained with sheer panic. "Rhys, Ben, engage the threat non-lethally! Create chaos! Scarlett, divert two rooftops east! We need to buy time for extraction!"

Scarlett didn't hesitate. She launched herself over the narrow gap between the bank roof and the adjacent commercial building, landing hard and rolling immediately behind a massive, humming air conditioning unit. The impact sent a dull throb through her recovering ribs, but the pain was instantly absorbed by the operational adrenaline.

She risked a glance down. The street below was now chaos. Rhys and Ben were executing the perfect non-lethal distraction: a staged collision involving their unmarked vehicle and a street-cleaning truck. Metal screamed, glass shattered, and civilians scattered. It was noisy, distracting, and provided the necessary cover.

"Comms Lead," she gasped, her voice tight with exertion. "LFO is two rooftops east. Need immediate extraction vector."

"Acknowledged. We are running contingency D. Move to the corner access ladder. Ben will meet you at street level, non-uniform," Arthur ordered, his voice regaining its terrifying, icy control. "Your extraction vehicle is a standard commercial taxi—white, Czech plates. Ben is the driver. Do not speak. Get in, lock the door, and secure the Ledger."

She followed the trajectory, moving with a feral intensity born of necessity. She found the rusted, exterior maintenance ladder and began her descent, the cold metal biting through her gloves.

As she reached the ground level—a narrow, refuse-strewn alley—a figure stepped directly into her path. He was tall, bulky, and wore a simple, dark utility jacket, devoid of identifying marks. He wasn't Rhys or Ben.

"Scarlett Harper?" the figure asked, his voice low, heavy, and speaking flawless English.

Her training took over. She didn't answer. She didn't hesitate. She pivoted hard, using the wall for leverage, and executed a perfect, non-lethal low-impact hip throw, dropping her attacker instantly onto the concrete beside a dumpster.

She heard a sharp curse in German as the man hit the ground, realizing instantly this was a high-value asset, likely Radek's own security detail. She didn't wait. She bolted towards the pre-arranged rendezvous point, running harder than she ever had before.

She saw the white taxi idling fifteen feet away, the driver—Ben, disguised in a simple denim jacket—scanning the alley nervously.

She lunged for the back door just as Ben threw it open.

"Get in, get in!" Ben yelled, his voice strained.

She collapsed into the vehicle just as the door slammed shut. The cab peeled out of the alley, instantly merging into the chaotic traffic.

"Status," she demanded, her hands already securing the digital injection kit.

"Clear for now. Rhys is covering the rear. Arthur is demanding a vitals report," Ben clipped, driving with controlled aggression.

Scarlett leaned back, taking a deep, shuddering breath. "Comms Lead, LFO is exfil. Ledger secured. Target neutralized non-lethally. Sending vitals now."

She had the Ledger. She was alive. But the raw, terrifying clarity of the fight and the exposure had stripped away the last veneer of safety. Her life was now a permanent, high-stakes game of evasion, command, and consequence.

Chapter 58: The Weight of the Ledger

The silence in the cottage was broken only by the sharp, ragged intake of Arthur's breath and the high-pitched static from the comms feed. 05:48. Scarlett was out. She was moving.

Arthur was staring at the telemetry monitor, his gaze locked on the fluctuating lines of her heart rate and the digital lock icon confirming the Ledger was secured. The adrenaline, which had been trapped in his immobile body for the last hour, was finally released in a massive, dizzying wave of exhaustion and relief. He was soaked in sweat, his limbs trembling with the residue of terror.

"Comms Lead to LFO," Arthur grated, pushing the comms button with a shaking finger. He kept his voice low, forcing a terrifying calm back into his tone. "Report status of Ledger data. Confirm injection point status."

"Comms Lead, this is LFO," Scarlett's voice was instantaneous in his earpiece, no longer strained, but sharp, immediate. "Ledger data secured on primary drive. Digital injection point is dead—manual withdrawal initiated before breach. Status: clear, Comms Lead. Ben is driving. ETA to safe house: forty-five minutes."

"Acknowledge, LFO. You're clear, Scarlett," Arthur confirmed, the use of her name a necessary breach of protocol. He slumped back against the sofa, letting the immediate, visceral pressure subside. He needed to process the intelligence, but the primary command—*survival*—had been met.

But survival wasn't enough.

He lunged for the secondary secure laptop, ignoring the searing protest of his fractured leg. He needed immediate confirmation on the threat.

"Comms Lead to Ben, report status of the subject neutralized in the alley," Arthur ordered, pulling up the Prague city surveillance feeds, using Deedee's secure injection method.

"Comms Lead, this is Ben. Subject was neutralized by the LFO with a non-lethal throw. He's Radek's security. Heavy, non-uniform. Subject is mobile but disoriented. Rhys is covering the clean-up," Ben reported, his voice steady against the sound of traffic.

Arthur scrubbed a hand over his face. "Acknowledged. LFO, that was high-value security. You exposed yourself with an unauthorized maneuver. Why?"

"Comms Lead, the asset compromised the exfil corridor. The neutralization was necessary to prevent a prolonged exchange and maintain the digital injection's cover integrity," Scarlett countered instantly, her professionalism unassailable. "I followed the training. I chose the path of least risk."

She was right. The logic was sound. She had neutralized a threat with skill and minimal exposure, something he was physically incapable of doing. The forced helplessness was the hardest reality to swallow.

He zoomed in on the city feed, focusing on the alley adjacent to Radek's bank. The clean-up was already underway: Rhys, disguised as municipal worker, was directing traffic around a staged delivery blockage. It was textbook field work.

"Arthur," Scarlett's voice was softer now, tinged with concern. "Report status. You're silent."

He forced a slow, steady exhale. "Status: stable, LFO. Analyzing threat matrix. We need eyes on the Mole."

The successful Prague extraction, while providing the digital Ledger, had confirmed the core threat was institutional, not physical. Gary, the Mole—they knew the *where* and the *when*. The local security asset was a symptom, not the cause.

"LFO, divert to the secondary protocol," Arthur instructed, his mind now racing through the contingency plans they had pre-loaded. "The Ledger data needs to be split immediately. Ben, access the secure drop location now. Scarlett, you are to physically remove the memory drive and store it on your person. Do not access the file again until you are back at the cottage."

He watched the GPS icon representing Scarlett's vehicle move steadily toward the designated secure drop location—a nondescript, pre-vetted Met safe house on the outskirts of the city. He needed the physical separation of the primary and secondary Ledger backup to prevent a simultaneous digital seizure.

"Comms Lead, LFO is stationary at the secure drop location," Ben reported, his voice dropping to a whisper. "Transferring data now. Primary drive removed and secured by the LFO."

"Confirmed. LFO, you are cleared for return journey. Maintain low comms until border crossing," Arthur instructed.

He leaned back, the high-resolution screens still burning into his retina. The silence returned to the cottage, no longer the oppressive dread of ingress, but the intense pressure of waiting.

He had the Ledger, split and secured. He had his wife, alive and in motion. But the Mole was still in play, Gary was still liquidating assets, and he was still tethered to a digital screen. He closed his eyes, forcing his analytical mind to focus on the next tactical phase: how to leverage the Ledger without exposing the LFO to the same risk twice. The cost of her competence was his continuing absence, and the thought was a searing, constant agony.

Chapter 59: The Weight of the Badge

The silence of the unmarked vehicle was a thick, heavy blanket, broken only by the low sound of the engine and the faint, controlled static of the comms feed. Scarlett was out of Prague, across the border, and moving steadily toward the initial rendezvous point. Her body was thrumming with residual adrenaline and the crushing fatigue of operational command.

She slumped against the passenger door, physically and emotionally spent. The Ledger—the digital file—was secured on a thumb drive in a hidden compartment of her vest. The drive felt impossibly small, yet carried the full, agonizing weight of their future: Arthur's career, Logan's safety, and the only leverage they had against Mr. Harper's global legal assault.

Ben, professional and silent, drove with controlled precision. He was the visible shield, but she knew the true shield was the man tethered to the screen in the cottage.

She pressed the comms mic, her voice barely a whisper. "Comms Lead, LFO is reporting physical status: stable. Vitals normalizing. Requesting personal comms for two minutes."

Arthur's voice, which had been tightly clipped and tactical throughout the journey, softened instantly. "Acknowledge, Scarlett. Personal comms enabled. Talk to me."

"It was... quiet," she confessed, the silence of the car allowing the raw edge of fear to surface. "Too quiet. Radek's security was high-value, not OCG thugs. They were waiting for a *digital* threat, not a physical one." She shuddered, recalling the moment the security guard appeared. "I had to use the hip throw. I hated it, Arthur. I hate that I'm good at it."

"You did exactly what you were trained for, Scarlett. You chose the path of least risk. You maintained cover integrity. You protected the Ledger. You were brilliant." His praise was sincere, but it was delivered with the terrifying knowledge that her brilliance put her in the path of the next bullet.

"But I was terrified of failing *you*," she admitted, the confession heavy. "Not the mission, not the file—failing you. Seeing your heart rate spike on my feed—I was the chaos you warned me against."

"You were human, Scarlett. I was the liability. I compromised the comms protocol. I broke my own stability. I need you to trust the operational reality, not my panic."

She closed her eyes, letting the truth settle. Arthur was confined, unable to be the physical shield he was trained to be. His love, his need to protect, was now a digital vulnerability, forcing her to be the unwavering anchor of command for both of them.

"I need to contact Logan," she said abruptly, the need to anchor herself in the domestic reality overriding the mission brief. "Just a quick, secure call to Jade. Just to hear him."

"Negative, LFO. Too risky. We maintain total comms darkness until the final drop point," Arthur countered instantly, the tactical boundary firm. "Jade confirms he's fine. He drew me a picture of the police van with a big spike on it. He's happy. You focus on the extraction."

The denial, however logical, felt like a cold, institutional wall. She was a mother, denied the comfort of her child's voice because she was wearing the operational badge.

"Understood, Comms Lead," she clipped, pushing the maternal ache down. The exchange had been brief, brutal, and necessary.

She spent the next hour reviewing the Ledger data she had injected into the secure laptop (the one Ben was running). The file confirmed everything: the vast scale of Radek's money laundering, the shell companies, and the deep, embedded connections running right back to Mr. Harper's legal firm—the absolute evidence they needed.

"Comms Lead," she reported, her voice regaining its legal clarity. "The Ledger confirms the entire financial network. Radek is the linchpin. The scale is staggering. This isn't just evidence for the custody case; this is a systemic takedown."

"Acknowledged. We hit them hard, Scarlett. We give this data directly to Deedee. This is the end of the line for Gary and the Mole," Arthur stated, his professional fire reignited by the tangible evidence.

She leaned back, watching the European countryside blur past the window. She was alive, she was operational, and she had the Ledger. But the price of command was immense: the agonizing terror of her husband's immobilization, the professional distance she had to maintain, and the crushing knowledge that the safety of her family now rested entirely on her ability to wear the badge.

Chapter 60: The Little Red Dress

Scarlett stood in the quiet sanctuary of the secure Met safe house near Prague, the cold reality of the new mission brief settling over her.

The Weapon: Red Silk and Exposed Skin

She was a vision of lethal, exposed desire: fire-engine red silk, a plunging neckline extending almost to her navel, and a deep V revealing her bare back, cut down almost to the tailbone. Her makeup was meticulously applied: sultry red lipstick matched the dress, and smoky eyes completed the goddess-in-red transformation. Her long hair, dyed to a shockingly bright blonde wig, cascaded down, framing her face and shoulders.

The Operational Hand-off (Comms)

"Soft acquisition," Deedee's voice confirmed via the secure comms link. "Cerberus is at the gala. Susceptible to vanity. You go in as Anastasia Radek, leveraging Radek's perceived downfall. Your job is to lead the target on, get him into a private setting, and ply him with a specialized, quick-acting compliance drug."

The air filled with the digital scream of Arthur's voice, his composure shattering instantly.

"NEGATIVE! ABSOLUTELY FUCKING NOT, DEEDEE! THAT IS A VIOLATION OF OPERATIONAL PARAMETERS AND A DIRECT THREAT TO MY WIFE! ABORT THE MISSION!"

Scarlett pressed the comms button, her voice dropping to a low, clear tone. "Arthur. Look at me. The decision is made, but this is us I'm fighting for. This is the last thing. I love you. It's you I'm coming home to, not the mission, not the Ledger."

The sincerity was absolute, yet Arthur's possessive control simply intensified. "I don't care about the cover! I care about the fact that every goddamn predatory animal in that room is going to be locked onto you! You think I don't see what that dress does? It's turning you into a target! It's exploitation!"

"I am risking my friends, Scarlett! Rhys and Ben are supposed to be your clean perimeter, and you're turning them into visual liabilities! They are human, and you are wearing a dress designed for conquest! You are taking an unnecessary risk with your own life just to prove a point, and that is not operational! That is reckless, self-serving chaos!"

"I am risking my life for the Ledger! And you are treating me like a civilian liability because you're scared!" Scarlett screamed, her voice tight with fury.

The Staging: The Knife and the Line

The door to the inner room opened, and Rhys and Ben, Arthur's close-protection detail, entered. They were charged with securing her discrete weapons.

It was during the staging that Arthur initiated the hidden camera—the lens showing the exposed reality of his wife among his friends. Rhys and Ben moved to her, their professional discomfort battling the necessity of securing the small, thin-bladed utility knife to her inner thigh.

Rhys knelt, securing the strap. His eyes, trained for detail, registered the perfect, uncompromised drape of the red silk against her skin.

"Scarlett," Rhys muttered, his voice barely a breath. "You're... not wearing anything beneath the dress."

"No, Rhys," Scarlett confirmed, her voice cold, operational. "The fabric is too fine. Any line, any seam, would compromise the cover profile. It would scream *security* or *fake*. The line can't be seen under the dress. We eliminate the line. Now, finish securing the asset."

Arthur, monitoring the internal feed, screamed into the comms channel.

"RHYS! BEN! YOU GET THE HELL OUT OF THAT ROOM NOW! I SEE YOU! YOU FUCKING LOOK AWAY FROM MY WIFE! SCARLETT! YOU ARE ABORTING THIS MISSION! YOU ARE BREAKING MY HEART!"

The rage hit Scarlett like a physical wave. The denial of her agency, the refusal to acknowledge her training, the constant reduction of her status to mere civilian broke her composure.

"I am not a civilian anymore, Arthur! I AM NOT A CIVILIAN ANYMORE!" she screamed into the mic, tears of fury springing to her eyes. "I am LFO! I am trained! I have been deployed! You are Comms! You follow my lead or you follow Deedee's rules!"

She snapped the comms unit off her throat. She looked straight into the lens of the hidden camera—the one she knew Arthur was viewing—her eyes hard, clear, and utterly cold.

"Too late, Arthur," she whispered. "LFO is mobile."

The Defiance: Drive to the Gala

Scarlett snatched the keys to the Ferrari Portofino and bolted from the safe house. She climbed into the car, the leather cool and luxurious.

Arthur's voice was silent now, but his panic still filled the air. She reached for the volume dial and slammed the high-fidelity speakers to maximum. The music was a tactical necessity, drowning out his fear.

The car's speakers filled the air with the defiant sound of a female voice: *"Oh, I'm just a girl living in captivity / Your rule of thumb make me worrisome / Oh, I'm just a girl, what's my destiny? / What I've succumbed to is making me numb."*

She switched the track. The atmosphere shifted immediately. The speakers now thundered with the dark, heavy, rhythmic roar of male voices, the lyrics a statement of her operational independence: *"Master of puppets are pulling the strings / Twisting your mind and smashing your dreams!"* The heavy, pounding beat matched the frantic rhythm of her heart, drowning out every last whisper of Arthur's terror and her own moral resistance.

She sped toward the city center, the powerful engine a vibrating pulse beneath her six-inch heels.

She reached the Prague Finance Gala just as the red carpet entrance was busiest. She drove the Ferrari straight into the entrance lane, stopping abruptly, ensuring every camera flash and every envious gaze was locked onto the devastating, exposed red silk.

Anastasia Radek emerged from the car: a vision of lethal, exposed red silk and cold blonde ambition. Her entrance wasn't subtle; it was a deliberate, stunning, operational declaration.

Come and find me, Cerberus, she thought, tossing the keys to the valet. *I'm the most desired woman in the room. And I'm ready to sell the soul of Radek's empire.*

Chapter 61: The Digital Inferno

The secure Comms Hub—Arthur's living room—was no longer a safe space; it was a torture chamber. Arthur, still propped on the sofa, surgical pins screaming against his rigid posture, watched the live feeds on his main monitor. His wife—his LFO—was making her entrance.

The Exposure: Red Silk and Command

The secondary camera feed, a discreet external unit Rhys had placed near the gala entrance, confirmed the nightmare in high-definition. Arthur saw the Ferrari Portofino screech to a halt. Then, Anastasia Radek emerged: the lethal, exposed column of fire-engine red silk, the plunging neckline, the bare back—a stunning, devastating portrait of operational vulnerability. He saw the deliberate, dramatic pause as she commanded the attention of every camera flash and every predatory eye.

His blood ran cold, instantly overriding the pain medication. He reached for the mute button on the main comms unit, but his fingers, slick with sweat, fumbled. He heard the dying echo of her operational defiance through the car's open window: the final, screaming lyrics of the heavy male voices, the absolute statement of her independence.

"She's inside," Arthur grated, his voice a raw whisper directed at the silent comms board. He was screaming into the void, cut off by her deliberate choice. "She's inside, and I can't even tell Rhys to follow her."

He was confined to the digital screen, forced to rely on the external camera network for eyes. Rhys and Ben—his trusted perimeter—were currently positioning themselves for unobtrusive observation outside the grand hall, their movements slow, controlled, and tragically inadequate for the chaos Scarlett had just initiated.

The Agony of Observation

Arthur zoomed in on the interior feed, leveraging the secure network to penetrate the gala's private CCTV. He found her almost instantly. She wasn't subtle; she was a beacon. She moved through the crowd with the deliberate, self-possessed swagger of the high-net-worth heir, making immediate, aggressive eye contact.

He watched the reaction of the crowd. It was instantaneous, animalistic. Every powerful man in the room—every potential OCG contact, every high-value target—gravitated toward the impossible vision in red. She was the most desired woman there, achieving the primary objective of the mission brief with terrifying speed.

But Arthur didn't see the operational success; he saw the exposure. He watched a prominent, known member of an Italian organized crime family track the line of her bare back with an unashamed leer. He watched Cerberus—a cold, middle-aged man known for his pathological control—break his conversation mid-sentence just to stare at the impossible plunge of the neckline.

"She's walking toward him," Arthur muttered, his fingers hovering uselessly over the inactive comms button. "She's initiating the soft acquisition. Cerberus is engaged."

Scarlett—Anastasia—stopped directly across the room from her target. She didn't approach him. She initiated the engagement using pure, non-verbal psychological warfare. She smiled, a cold, calculated, confident smile that spoke volumes about her availability and her ambition. She turned her body, presenting the devastating line of the exposed back and the impossible height of the heels, before pivoting back to accept a glass of champagne from a waiter.

Cerberus broke first. He abandoned his conversation and walked directly toward her.

"He's taking the bait," Arthur whispered, slamming his fist onto the arm of the sofa, the pain a welcome distraction from the psychological anguish. "Target is engaged. LFO is in the acquisition phase."

The Blackmail and the Breach

The tension intensified as the conversation began. Arthur had no audio feed, only lip-reading and body language. He watched them talk for five minutes. Cerberus was visibly hooked, his posture shifting from cautious interest to aggressive, predatory pursuit.

Scarlett played the role of the ambitious heir perfectly, occasionally touching Cerberus's arm with casual intimacy, leaning in to whisper a confidence that allowed the bright blonde hair to fall, obscuring her face and adding to the mystique.

Then, the final stage of the acquisition. Cerberus took her hand and led her away from the main gala floor, toward the private, secure offices on the mezzanine.

"She's moving to the private setting," Arthur barked, initiating the secondary comms unit—the emergency, unauthorized channel connected directly to Deedee. "Deedee, LFO is moving to the compliance stage. Estimated time to breach: ten minutes. I need a clean perimeter sweep of that mezzanine floor *now*."

He watched the last image of her—a goddess in lethal red, disappearing behind the dark wood paneling—before she was lost to the internal CCTV coverage.

"I need eyes, Deedee," Arthur pleaded, the voice of the husband cracking through the tactical calm. "I need confirmation she's not alone. That psychopath is going to lock that door, and I'm six hundred miles away, watching a fucking silent screen."

The agony of his immobilization—his complete and utter lack of control over the safety of the woman who held his heart—was the final, crushing sentence. He could only wait for the comms signal that would confirm the use of the compliance drug, the sound of the utility knife securing the asset, or, worst of all, the sound of silence.

Chapter 62: The Soft Acquisition

The private office on the mezzanine level was everything the gala floor wasn't: quiet, sterile, and dominated by heavy, dark wood. Scarlett—Anastasia—felt the door click shut behind her. She was alone with the target, Mr. Krosnik.

The Compliance Protocol

Mr. Krosnik immediately locked the office door and turned to her, his eyes dark with predatory confidence. He saw reckless ambition in her red silk and sharp heels, a willingness to play a high-stakes game he believed he had already won.

"Anastasia," he murmured, his voice thick with satisfied expectation. "I admire your directness. Let's discuss this investment over something less public."

Scarlett knew the time for subtlety was over. She maintained eye contact, letting her lips curve into the cold, calculated smile of the heir.

"Of course," she purred. "But first, a proper toast. To new partnerships, Mr. Krosnik."

She reached immediately for the champagne flute she had carried, subtly palming the custom-made compliance capsule concealed beneath her red lipstick. She moved with practiced grace, pouring the champagne, her bare back deliberately presented to him as she feigned a search for an appropriate space.

As he reached for the flute, she executed the transfer: a quick, practiced flick of her thumb, releasing the contents of the capsule into his glass. She immediately raised her own flute, clinking it against his.

"To the Ledger," she whispered, watching him drink deeply.

The Psychological Edge

The drug—a high-concentration benzodiazepine analogue—was designed to be rapid. They talked for five agonizing minutes, Mr. Krosnik growing increasingly bold, his eyes fixed on the impossible plunge of her neckline.

"You don't talk like a lawyer, Anastasia," he slurred slightly, the first sign of the drug taking hold. "You talk like a predator."

"Takes one to know one," she countered.

Suddenly, his eyes narrowed, and a hint of caution—the professional predator recognizing a threat—crept back into his gaze.

"This is moving too fast," he murmured, trying to reassert command. "I don't know who you work for."

Scarlett knew she had to eliminate his suspicion. She executed the move perfectly: she slowly uncrossed her legs, letting the red silk split open slightly, then crossed them again, ensuring the brief, intentional flash of bare skin confirmed the absence of underwear. She held his gaze and bit her bright red lips, a gesture of aggressive invitation.

His focus shattered. His suspicion dissolved into raw, aggressive lust. He reached for her, his control dissolving entirely. His touch was clumsy, predictable. Scarlett allowed the contact, maintaining eye contact, waiting for the precise moment of physical compliance. As his grasp softened—a subtle, almost imperceptible falter in his muscle tension—she pivoted.

She guided him toward the heavy, leather sofa. He collapsed, no longer resisting, his eyes fluttering, his body heavy and pliant.

The silence returned, cold and thick. Scarlett was safe. The compliance window was open.

"Comms Lead," she whispered into the mic, her voice tight with professional strain. "LFO is secure. Target is compliant. Initiating extraction protocol."

Arthur's voice was instantaneous in her ear, sharp and laced with relief. "Status confirmed, LFO. Heart rate 140 bpm. You are pushing the compliance window. You have twenty minutes, Scarlett. Access his comms now. Did you just fucking Sharon Stone him?"

Scarlett didn't allow the flicker of humor the question afforded. "It worked, didn't it," she clipped back, her voice all business. "Rhys and Ben are moving to the interior corridor for breach cover."

The Digital Extraction

Scarlett knelt, her silk dress pooling around her, accessing Mr. Krosnik's encrypted mobile.

"Krosnik," she commanded, her voice low and sharp, leveraging the drug's influence. "Access. Now. Secondary comms. PINs and passwords."

Mr. Krosnik mumbled, compliant, his mind trapped between lust and pharmacological haze. "Pretty girl... you're a good little worker, aren't you? Such a good little girl... I like that in an asset." He slurred out a complex, multi-digit PIN. "You're going to make a lot of money, sweet thing."

Scarlett ignored the vile words, her fingers flying to input the code.

"Krosnik, secondary password. Travel and logistics files. Speak clearly."

"Password is... the day I met your mother, sweet thing," he chuckled, the misogyny sickening. He gave her a four-digit number. "You remind me of her. Less *prude*, though."

Scarlett bypassed the first layer of authentication using the codes he willingly provided. She needed his final destination.

Extraction Objective 1: Travel Itinerary.

"Comms Lead, I have the authentication. He's willingly giving up the data. Accessing travel logs."

She accessed his encrypted calendar. "I have a flight scheduled for Istanbul, 07:00. Private jet. Primary extraction route secured: Service Exit Delta."

"Acknowledge, LFO! That is high-value intelligence! Get out, Scarlett! You have met the objective!" Arthur screamed, his voice breaking with urgency.

But Scarlett couldn't stop. She saw a file labeled "LOGISTICS_G". She accessed it, the content flashing across the screen: coordinates, code names, and a final, sickening confirmation.

The Ledger was secondary. The immediate threat was real. She had to secure the final piece of the tactical puzzle.

Chapter 63: The Price of Exposure

The silence of the service alley was instantly replaced by the terrifying, deafening roar of shattered glass. "LOGISTICS_G".

Scarlett's fingers flew, ripping the memory drive containing the Ledger from Krosnik's phone and stuffing it into the hidden lumbar sheath. The Ledger was secondary; survival was absolute.

"Comms Lead," Arthur's voice screamed in her earpiece, shattering the silence. "Target is compromised! They were monitoring the primary lock! Get out! Move! Move!"

Scarlett ignored the escalating panic in her ear. She instantly smashed the comms device against the desk, silencing the immediate input. She launched herself off the floor, overturning the heavy mahogany chair as a momentary barrier. The tight red silk dress immediately restricted her movement, the six-inch Jimmy Choos already kicked off.

She drew the thin-bladed utility knife from the small of her back. The first man lunged. She used the knife, not to kill, but to create immediate, debilitating damage—a deep slice across his forearm. He roared, stumbling back. She immediately drew the second knife, countering the second attacker's heavy punch with a swift, horizontal slice across his thigh, compromising his mobility.

She didn't pause for the door. She sprinted toward the huge, ornate window overlooking the main financial street. She wrapped her silk-clad elbow and forearm in the heavy drapery and smashed the glass outwards.

The sound of shattering glass tore through the mezzanine level. Scarlett didn't hesitate. She threw her body over the ledge, rappelling down the sheer side of the building onto the narrow, ornate ledge of the floor below. The unforgiving silk tore with a long, satisfying rip up the side—releasing her legs for movement.

Thank God I was duct-taped into this thing, she thought, the dark humor a necessary shield against the terror.

She hit the ground—a narrow, refuse-strewn service alley—and sprinted toward the waiting Ferrari Portofino.

She lunged into the driver's seat. Her fingers, slick with sweat and adrenaline, found the key. The engine roared to life.

The alley exit was instantly blocked by a dark, heavy sedan, its passengers dismounting with weapons drawn.

Scarlett slammed the gear selector into reverse, the expensive sports car protesting the rough handling. She spun the wheel, executing a perfect 180-degree turn, the silk dress bunched around her.

She slammed the gear selector forward, hitting the main financial street. The streets, still slick and busy from the rush of the gala traffic, were now her tactical playground.

A frantic voice—Rhys, overriding the emergency comms protocol—broke through the residual static of the local radio.

"LFO! This is Rhys! You've got two tails! Red Mercedes and a black Audi! They are on you! You have to evade them now, Scarlett! You have to break the line!"

Scarlett gripped the leather wheel, the blood pounding in her ears. Arthur's voice, still audible despite the smashed comms unit, was a constant, raw stream of tactical panic and personal terror: *"Turn left! Left, damn it! You're exposing your flank! Abort! Abort the line!"*

She reached for the volume dial, slamming the high-fidelity speakers to maximum. The music was a tactical necessity, drowning out his fear and restoring her focus.

The car speakers instantly filled with the aggressive, driving beat of a male voice, the lyrics defiant and familiar: *"This is the perfect way to die!"*

She laughed, the sound raw and exhilarating. "You mean a car chase, Rhys? I've always wanted to do this!"

She switched the track again, needing a rhythm she could map her movements to. The speakers roared with a heavy, driving male voice, instantly hitting a soaring, familiar melody: *"I was made for loving you, baby!"* The music was an immediate, powerful shield against Arthur's remote panic.

The chase was on. The Ferrari was built for speed, and Scarlett—unrestricted by the torn silk and free of the impossible heels—drove with a desperate, feral intensity.

She utilized the precise, rhythmic structure of the music to time her maneuvers. As the chorus hit its high point, she slammed the wheel left, narrowly avoiding a civilian vehicle, the car engine singing against the soaring vocal line. She mapped her evasion to the simple, irresistible bassline: *"Do, do, do, da, do, do, do, da, do."*

She wove the car through the narrow streets, using the tight, rhythmic pulse of the song to guide her decisions. She hit a sharp, wet corner as the voice soared, perfectly timing the drift, throwing the tailing vehicles into momentary disarray. The taunt was digital, the execution physical: *"I was made for loving you, baby!"*

The pursuit was relentless. The tailing vehicles, clearly built for brute force, were struggling with the Ferrari's agility. Scarlett pushed the speed, knowing her primary advantage was the car's handling and the sheer absurdity of the high-speed chase cutting through the quiet, post-gala streets.

She heard Arthur's distant, frantic voice—a ghost in her ear—trying to break through the operational shield she had built. *"Scarlett, pull over! You're going to lose control! You're not trained for this!"*

She laughed again, slamming the car into a daring gap between a city bus and a delivery van, the heavy rhythm of the music guiding the precision of her movements. She wasn't trained for this; she was *made* for this chaos. The rhythm of the song was the operational brief she needed, focusing her terror into absolute, kinetic control.

She pushed the car harder, faster, the music a deafening, exhilarating command. She had the Ledger. She had the asset. She had the mission. And she was going to drive this beautiful, terrifying machine until the music stopped.

Chapter 64: The Remote Lead

The cottage living room was an operational war zone. The digital light of the secure monitors—now showing multiple, chaotic, fragmented street feeds from Prague—was the only illumination. Arthur was pressed against the sofa cushions, his fractured leg screaming in protest, his entire focus consumed by the pixelated red blur that was the Ferrari. He was the Remote Tactical Lead, but he was drowning in the sheer, overwhelming chaos his wife had unleashed.

He had retrieved the smashed comms unit and connected it to the external speaker, allowing Rhys and Ben's frantic instructions to fill the air. But the primary reality was the music. It was a tactical shield and a personal torment, drowning out every professional command he tried to issue.

"I was made for loving you, baby!" The heavy, relentless rhythm was a constant, deafening reminder of her defiance.

Arthur slammed his fist onto the armrest. "Rhys! Get a visual on the tailing vehicles! I need plate numbers!

She's running blind, and she has the Ledger! Tell her to *slow down*!"

"Comms Lead, this is Rhys! We've lost visual on the Ferrari! The Audi and the Mercedes are still on vector! They're pushing civilian traffic!" Rhys's voice was ragged with panic. "The LFO's driving is... aggressive, Comms Lead! She's using the city buses as cover!"

Arthur zoomed in on a high-angle building camera feed, tracking the red flicker between the towering, baroque architecture. He saw the daring, insane maneuver as she slammed the car into a narrow gap, perfectly timed to the chaotic rhythm of the music.

"She's not running blind, Rhys," Arthur grated, his voice tight with a terrifying mix of fury and immense, unwanted pride. "She's using the music's tempo to map her evasions! She's turning the city into a goddamn drum kit! Focus on the tails!"

The terror wasn't just the pursuit; it was the chilling, professional precision of the two tailing vehicles. They weren't police; they were mercenaries. And they were operating with impossible speed and coordination.

"The Mole," Arthur whispered, the truth a bitter taste in his mouth. "They knew the Ledger was compromised. They knew the compliance window. They were waiting for her to surface."

He accessed the secondary, secure laptop, pulling up the communication logs from the Prague staging area. He didn't trust Deedee's unit anymore—not since the institutional corruption had been confirmed. The Mole wasn't just leaking data; they were running the counter-operation.

"Comms Lead to Rhys, divert immediately! I need you to run a perimeter sweep on the secondary drop location now! I suspect the extraction point is compromised! Do not engage!" Arthur ordered, overriding Rhys's request for a clear intercept vector.

Arthur knew the mission brief inside out. Scarlett's designated safety house—a pre-vetted Met apartment—was the most obvious extraction point. If the Mole was running the counter-op, they would have assets waiting there.

He focused on the comms log. He needed to identify the leak. He scanned the time stamps of the final communication logs: the time Scarlett confirmed the

Ledger was secured, the time Rhys reported the tails, and the critical five-minute window in between.

There it was: a single, encrypted ping originated from within the secure Met network, routed through a satellite dish in a neutral country, immediately following Scarlett's initial comms check after the Ledger retrieval. It was a beacon. It was a digital map showing the enemy exactly where to go.

"The Mole is Comms, Deedee's internal support," Arthur deduced aloud, his voice low and cold. "They waited for her to retrieve the asset, then flagged the Ferrari's GPS line."

He stared at the monitor, his gaze catching the fleeting image of Scarlett's face—barefoot, hair flying, eyes blazing with a feral, exhilarating focus. She wasn't fighting for protocols; she was fighting for the Ledger, for their safety, and for the sheer, defiant act of survival.

He switched his focus back to the pursuit. The Ferrari was weaving through a crowded market square, the melody of the song hitting its high, soaring peak.

"LFO, listen to me," Arthur commanded, picking up the separate comms mic and overriding the music's volume, if only for a second. "Abort the house! The house is burned! Take the river bridge! The river bridge is the only chance to lose the line!"

He had no way of knowing if she heard him. The music roared back, a triumphant, defiant command.

Arthur forced himself to breathe. He couldn't trust the Met's extraction points, he couldn't trust the comms unit, and he couldn't trust his own legs. He had to trust Scarlett's instinct and the chaos she controlled so beautifully. He had to find a clean extraction point himself, one that the Mole—whoever they were—couldn't anticipate.

He was the Remote Tactical Lead, and his operational marriage was currently driving a stolen Ferrari toward an unsanctioned rendezvous.

Chapter 65: The Break and the Burn

The Immediate Aftermath

The silence of the unmarked vehicle was a thick, heavy blanket, broken only by the low sound of the engine and the controlled crackle of static. Scarlett was out of Prague, across the border, and moving steadily toward the initial rendezvous point. She slumped against the passenger door, physically and emotionally spent.

She reached for the secondary, discreet radio Rhys had insisted on for local communication. "LFO to Perimeter. Report status and position. I am at grid alpha-seven. Do you copy?"

The response was instantaneous, crackling with relief. "LFO, this is Rhys! We copy! Thank Christ! We're at grid alpha-nine, moving to intercept. We've lost the tails. We need to clear the asset immediately. Stay put!"

Five minutes later, Rhys and Ben pulled up in the unmarked vehicle. They moved with desperate, controlled speed, pulling Scarlett from the blood-splattered Ferrari.

"You're alive," Ben muttered, his focus strictly operational as he began wiping down the Ferrari for prints.

"Ledger secure, Rhys. Digital extraction only," Scarlett confirmed, ripping open her vest and handing over the memory drive.

Rhys secured the drive to his own person. He looked at the devastating silk dress and the raw exhaustion beneath the heavy makeup. "Scarlett, you went dark on comms. Why?"

"The primary comms were compromised. I destroyed the unit as soon as I heard the breach," Scarlett stated. "But before I did, I heard something in my ear—a voice on the channel, running interference. It wasn't Arthur, it wasn't Ben, and it wasn't you. It was static, a burst of sound that cut across the main line. It was a digital anomaly, but it was *human*."

Rhys and Ben exchanged a look that solidified the terror. The digital anomaly confirmed the Mole was active, running the counter-operation directly against them.

"The extraction house is burned," Rhys finished, his face grim. "Arthur was already warning us. He must have seen the ping when you secured the Ledger. The Mole knew the destination."

"Then we can't trust any of the pre-vetted Met safe houses," Ben confirmed, slamming the Ferrari door shut. "We're running unsanctioned, and the institutional threat knows our playbook."

Ditching the Mask

Scarlett didn't wait for instruction. The elaborate disguise that had been her operational shield was now a massive, flashing vulnerability. The people chasing the Ferrari were hunting a blonde in a distinctive red gown.

She ripped the blonde wig from her head, letting her dark, natural hair spill over her shoulders. The immediate removal felt like shedding an identity. She used a wet wipe from the glove box to ruthlessly scrub the sultry red lipstick and smoky eyes from her face, leaving her exhausted, bruised features bare.

Rhys caught the hint instantly. "The pub, LFO. High traffic. We need to disappear the red silk now."

"We need high civilian traffic to disappear, but that uniform is... a distraction," Ben began, looking at the devastated silk dress with the huge, accidental, high leg slit.

"The distraction is the mission," Scarlett clipped, already calculating the advantage. "No one looks for a fugitive in a six-figure gown at a local pub. They look for tactical gear."

The Unsanctioned Skill

Rhys turned back to Scarlett, a slow, genuine smile spreading across his face, replacing the tension. "Before we discuss high-level institutional corruption, we need a technical debrief. That driving, Scarlett. You turned that Ferrari into a goddamn torpedo. Where in God's name did a solicitor learn to drive like that?"

Scarlett allowed herself a small, exhausted smile, a moment of raw, personal truth piercing the professional shell. "That? That was nothing. I used to steal and joyride my dad's cars all the time when I was a kid. Fast corners, tight gaps—it was the only way I could get out of the house. I've always wanted to do that, actually."

Rhys barked a laugh—a loud, genuine sound of relief and shock. "A solicitor who joyrides. Arthur is going to kill you, but that initiative saved our lives."

"He's already trying to," Scarlett muttered, referencing the destroyed comms unit.

The Pivot: A Public Sanctuary

"The safe house is dead, but we need a clean rendezvous point. Now," Rhys commanded. "Arthur needs a clean channel for ten minutes to find us new assets. We need high civilian traffic and anonymity."

They found a busy local pub—all dark wood, low lighting, and high civilian density—the perfect spot for a brief, public sanctuary. Rhys and Ben formed an immediate, unobtrusive perimeter while Scarlett found a booth in the quietest corner. She immediately connected the encrypted satellite phone to Arthur.

Arthur's voice, sharp and immediate, filled her ear, laced with a familiar, immense relief. "Scarlett! Thank God! I saw the pursuit drop, but the Mole is working too fast. I've been running the contingency plans for an hour. I need ten minutes to vet a clean house. Stay put. Do not move. And tell me what the hell happened to the comms unit!"

Scarlett looked down at the devastating garment. The ripped, very high leg slit was now permanent, and the dress had become a bold, contradictory testament to her operational chaos.

She had been sitting for less than five minutes when the traffic began. The pub, previously focused on football and cheap beer, seemed to pivot its entire focus to her. Men—a stream of them, young and old, polished and rough—began approaching her table.

"Are you waiting for someone, darling? We haven't seen a dress like that in here in a long time."

"That silk is wasted on this corner, love. Can I get you a drink?"

"Your heels are missing, I can buy you better ones, princess."

Scarlett met every gaze with the cold, professional smile. She was using her accidental exposure as an operational shield, leading every potential threat on, ensuring the eyes of the city were locked entirely onto the goddess in red, not the two silent men guarding the exits.

She was the LFO, and the cost of her mission was measured not just in bullets, but in the agony of public, exposed desire.

Chapter 66: The Tethered Terror

The Command Center Crisis

Arthur was hunched over the secure laptops, the screens blazing in the dark cottage, his fractured leg braced stiffly against the sofa. The adrenaline spike from the escape and the subsequent comms break had left him shaking with a toxic cocktail of fury and relief. He was operating on pure, desperate necessity.

The satellite phone—the untraceable, heavy piece of emergency tech—was pressed to his ear. The pub noise, muffled by distance, filled the line.

"Scarlett, I hear the background feed," Arthur grated, his voice raw from the exertion of managing the crisis. "The pub is hot. You have two minutes before Rhys needs to move you. What is the composition of the threat in that room?"

"Comms Lead, the composition is civilian, localized, and currently compliant," Scarlett's voice was clear, crisp, and maddeningly calm. "I am the visual shield. Rhys and Ben are maintaining the perimeter. But the distraction is temporary. You need to pull us to a *clean* asset, Arthur. Something outside the Met's approved playbook."

Arthur slammed his free hand onto the armrest. "I know! The Mole is too deep! They knew the safe house vector! I'm running deep searches on SR (Special Reconnaissance) assets now—old contacts who owe me favors, who exist outside the institutional sphere!"

His gaze swept across the main monitor, where a secondary feed, routed through Rhys's discreet pocket camera, confirmed his wife's insane exposure. He saw the dark, crowded pub, the endless stream of male attention, and the impossible contradiction that was Scarlett. The contrast between her dark, exhausted face and the scandalous, ripped red silk dress was a visceral torment.

"Rhys, intercept the subject. Non-lethal disengagement. Now," Arthur commanded.

"Comms Lead, subject disengaged. LFO maintained cover integrity," Rhys reported, his tone strained.

The Continental Vector Asset

"I need a clean asset, Arthur," Scarlett urged, the noise of the pub filling the line. "Vegas rules. No paper trail. Something unsanctioned. We need transport back to the UK line, something that won't flag a customs database."

Arthur found it. A retired colleague, a former SAS technical specialist named 'Rico,' who ran a highly discrete vehicle recovery and transport business operating between Germany and the Czech Republic. Rico owed Arthur a marker from a disastrous mission in Bosnia ten years prior—a marker Arthur had sworn he would never cash. Rico specialized in moving assets and high-value, unsanctioned materials across borders.

"LFO, divert to Munich. I am routing the travel vector now," Arthur instructed, his fingers flying across the keyboard to send the encrypted coordinates to Rhys's vehicle GPS. "The asset is unsanctioned. Rico. He owes me a life. He runs a secure transport workshop near Munich. No paper trail, no institutional flags. He can arrange transport and clean papers for the continental land route. It's the cleanest line we have."

"Munich?" Scarlett questioned, the calm breaking slightly. "That's a long, exposed land route, Arthur. That's high-risk for customs and border patrol."

"It's the only place the Mole won't anticipate. They'll be watching airfields, borders, and Met safe houses," Arthur countered, his voice hard. "You need a physical buffer, Scarlett. You need to disappear, and Rico's transport line is a black hole for paperwork. You need to confirm the risk and accept the asset."

Scarlett didn't hesitate. "Confirmed. LFO is accepting the new asset and vector. Initiate comms hand-off to Rhys."

The Digital Leash

Arthur initiated the handover, transferring the Comms Lead role for the ground journey to Rhys, who could provide a more stable link while driving. But Arthur kept the primary telemetry running.

He focused on the pub feed for the final moments of her extraction. He saw Rhys and Ben execute the disengagement, seamlessly blending into the crowd, pulling Scarlett into the stream of foot traffic. She didn't look back at the men she had so easily acquired as a shield. She simply became a dark-haired woman in a badly ripped, ridiculously expensive red dress, disappearing into the street noise.

Arthur leaned back, closing his eyes. The screens were now showing a moving vehicle icon heading southwest toward the German border. He was useless again—condemned to monitor her vital signs and the agonizingly slow progress of her unsanctioned extraction.

He was the Remote Tactical Lead, and his entire operational existence was now a digital leash tied to the woman who loved chaos more than compliance.

Chapter 67: The Continental Run

The Land Route

The shift from the frantic energy of the Prague pub to the confined silence of the unmarked vehicle was jarring. Scarlett was huddled in the back seat, the remnants of the red silk dress covered now by a drab, heavy-duty blanket Rhys had provided. The sophisticated disguise was gone, replaced by the grim reality of exhaustion and the scent of cold fear.

"Comms Lead is running the first check," Rhys clipped, his eyes focused on the GPS display now showing the trajectory toward Munich. "Arthur confirmed the border protocols. We move fast. Rico's drop point is just outside Munich, ETA eight hours."

Scarlett pressed the comms button, her voice low. "Comms Lead, LFO is mobile. Confirming route acceptance. What is the status of the Mole?"

Arthur's voice, sharp and immediate, was her only link to stability. "The Mole is silent. That means they know you're mobile and they're waiting for your *next* point of failure. Rico's location is secure, but the land route is exposed. I need you running constant visual checks. Nothing is mundane, Scarlett. Not on this line."

She spent the next three hours running the visual checks he demanded, her training overriding her fatigue. She wasn't just looking for tailing vehicles; she was scanning for anomalies—unusual patterns in traffic flow, parked cars too close to overpasses, or the subtle presence of long-range surveillance. The sheer emptiness of the continental highway, interspersed with highly controlled border zones, was a perfect breeding ground for paranoia.

The Exposure of Command

The physical strain was immense. The residual effects of the compliance drug, combined with the adrenaline crash from the car chase, left her shaky and nauseous. Yet, she found a terrible kind of focus in the exhaustion. She was the Lead Field Operative, and Rhys and Ben were executing *her* extraction plan.

She realized how acutely aware her perimeter team was of the tension between her and Arthur. Rhys, while professional, often glanced at the useless primary comms unit, a silent acknowledgement of the power vacuum she now occupied.

"The Mole is targeting command, LFO," Ben stated quietly, pulling her focus back to the road. "They hit the comms unit and the safe house simultaneously. They knew Arthur was immobile, and they knew you were disposable—until you proved you weren't."

"They know the Met's SOPs," Scarlett murmured, running the analysis. "They hit the predictable targets. Our advantage is now chaos and the unsanctioned asset. Rico is our chaos."

She accessed the encrypted Ledger file on the secondary laptop, ignoring the headache that throbbed behind her eyes. "I need data on the logistical targets between here and Munich. Radek's digital files confirmed two key distribution points on this route. They are backup liquidation targets for Gary."

Rhys acknowledged instantly, pulling up the map display. "Target Alpha is a vehicle inspection depot. Target Beta is a small logistics warehouse outside Stuttgart. Too predictable for the Ledger, but they might hold operational assets."

"We move too fast for a digital strike," Scarlett concluded. "But we hit Target Alpha. We need to confirm if the Mole has compromised their local comms or assets. We leave a silent marker for Deedee—a ghost trail."

The Burden of Leadership

The necessity of the mission outweighed the risk of exposure. They were running on fumes, but they were running with purpose.

"LFO, the vehicle inspection depot is three klicks ahead," Rhys announced. "We hit the security feed and drop a trace? Or we go loud?"

"Loud is a breach. We hit the security feed," Scarlett instructed, the cold clarity of command settling over her. "Ben, prep the digital interface. We want to see who's watching the surveillance feed. Rhys, maintain the perimeter. We're in and out in ninety seconds."

She felt a moment of deep, visceral exhaustion. She was ordering two highly trained operatives—operatives Arthur had personally vouched for—into a high-risk scenario while relying entirely on a strategy conceived in terror. Yet, she had no choice. She was the LFO, and the weight of command was hers alone.

Chapter 68: The Price of a Marker

The Remote Command

The secure cottage was silent save for the hum of the servers. Arthur, the strategic command, was operating on raw, exhausting necessity, tethered to the digital world.

The satellite phone—the heavy, untraceable tech—was pressed to his ear. The immediate chaos of the Prague pub was behind them, replaced by the strategic silence of the open road.

"Jacobs here," Arthur grated, using his professional surname to anchor the command. "Rhys, confirm speed and border checkpoint status."

"Comms Lead, this is Rhys. Speed confirmed. Holding stable. Crossing into Germany in thirty. We bypassed the standard customs line. We're clean for now," Rhys's voice was crisp and controlled over the ground comms.

Arthur's gaze swept across the main monitor, where the telemetry feed showed Scarlett's vitals stabilizing—a fact that offered a small, necessary measure of relief.

"Acknowledge. LFO, confirm physical status. And check your secondary storage," Arthur instructed, his voice hardening into the objective tone of command. He knew she was no longer in the pub; she was in the containment phase.

"Comms Lead, LFO confirms stable. Physical discomfort minimal. Ledger drive secure in the lumbar sheath," Scarlett affirmed, her voice clear, professional, and devoid of the fatigue he knew she felt.

The Strategic Handover

Arthur knew the necessity of this operational structure. He was the immobile strategic brain, confined to vetting the unsanctioned asset (Rico) and monitoring the institutional threat (the Mole). Rhys was the tactical field comms and immediate protection lead.

"Rhys, I am routing the final coordinates for Rico's facility now. It's an isolated transport warehouse outside Munich. The rendezvous is non-negotiable. It's the last clean line we have," Arthur ordered. "Once you meet Rico, you hand off the LFO and Ben to his transport. You and your vehicle are immediately compromised and must initiate a secondary exfil for cover."

"Understood, Comms Lead. We'll burn the trail," Rhys confirmed.

Arthur focused on Scarlett. He needed to anchor her once more before the long digital separation of the continental drive. He bypassed the tactical chatter to speak directly to her.

"Scarlett, listen to me," Arthur demanded, using her name to ground the command. "Rico is a massive marker. We are entirely unsanctioned on this line. You are crossing three international borders. Your focus is singular: Asset transfer and security. Do not engage local law enforcement. Do not, under any circumstances, compromise Rico or his business."

"Understood, Jacobs. We acquire the transport and disappear," she affirmed.

The Romantic Anchor

He knew the professional briefing was complete, but the husband needed one final, quiet confirmation. He lowered his voice, pulling the satellite phone slightly away from the comms hub.

"I need a moment, LFO," Arthur admitted, the strain in his voice apparent. "I hate this. I hate that I'm here, and you are running."

Scarlett's voice immediately softened, the professional operative yielding to the partner. "I know, Arthur. But I need you to be the only person who can stop the Mole. I need you to be safe. And I miss my husband, Arthur. And I need you to be waiting for me."

"I'll be waiting. And I'll find a way to burn every single one of those dresses," he promised, the threat laced with fierce, desperate tenderness.

Arthur ended the comms link, the sudden silence leaving him breathless. He looked at the main monitor, where the moving vehicle icon hurtled toward Munich. He was useless again—condemned to monitor her vital signs and the agonizingly slow progress of her unsanctioned extraction.

Chapter 69: The Strategic Silence

The Remote Command

The secure cottage was silent save for the hum of the servers. Arthur, the strategic command, was operating on raw, exhausting necessity, tethered to the digital world. The heavy satellite phone was pressed to his ear.

"Jacobs here," Arthur grated, using his professional surname to anchor the command. "Rhys, confirm current operational status and distance from Munich vector."

"Comms Lead, this is Rhys. Status green. We're holding speed at optimal cruise. We're past the primary border checkpoints and maintaining cover integrity. Current distance to Rico's staging area is seven hours, forty minutes," Rhys's voice was crisp and controlled over the ground comms.

Arthur's gaze swept across the main monitor, where the telemetry feed showed Scarlett's vitals stabilizing—a fact that offered a small, necessary measure of relief.

"Acknowledge. LFO, confirm physical status. And check your secondary storage," Arthur instructed, his voice hardening into the objective tone of command.

"Comms Lead, LFO confirms stable. Physical discomfort minimal. Ledger drive secure in the lumbar sheath," Scarlett affirmed, her voice clear, professional, and devoid of the fatigue he knew she felt.

The Strategic Handover

Arthur knew the necessity of this operational structure. He was the immobile strategic brain, confined to vetting the unsanctioned asset (Rico) and monitoring the institutional threat (the Mole). Rhys was the tactical field comms and immediate protection lead.

"Rhys, maintain strict discipline. The ground link is our most exposed asset. Checkpoints are fluid on the continental line. No stops. You are running unsanctioned. Once you meet Rico, you hand off the LFO and Ben to his transport. You and your vehicle are immediately compromised and must initiate a secondary exfil for cover."

"Understood, Comms Lead. We'll burn the trail," Rhys confirmed.

Arthur focused on Scarlett. He needed to anchor her once more before the long digital separation of the continental drive. He bypassed the tactical chatter to speak directly to her.

"Scarlett, listen to me," Arthur demanded, using her name to ground the command. "Rico is a massive marker. We are entirely unsanctioned on this line. You are crossing three international borders. Your focus is singular: Asset transfer and security. Do not engage local law enforcement. Do not, under any circumstances, compromise Rico or his business."

"Understood, Jacobs. We acquire the transport and disappear," she affirmed.

The Romantic Anchor

He knew the professional briefing was complete, but the husband needed one final, quiet confirmation. He lowered his voice, pulling the satellite phone slightly away from the comms hub.

"I need a moment, LFO," Arthur admitted, the strain in his voice apparent. "I hate this. I hate that I'm here, and you are running."

Scarlett's voice immediately softened, the professional operative yielding to the partner. "I know, Arthur. But I need you to be the only person who can stop the Mole. I need you to be safe. And I miss my husband, Arthur. And I need you to be waiting for me."

"I'll be waiting. And I'll find a way to burn every single one of those dresses," he promised, the threat laced with fierce, desperate tenderness.

Arthur ended the comms link, the sudden silence leaving him breathless. He looked at the main monitor, where the moving vehicle icon hurtled toward Munich. He was useless again—condemned to monitor her vital signs and the agonizingly slow progress of her unsanctioned extraction.

Chapter 70: Triage on the Road

The Operational Burden

The interior of the unmarked vehicle was a cocoon of tactical tension. Hours had melted into the German highway system, far past the initial border crossing. Scarlett was huddled in the back, the low hum of the engine and the controlled crackle of the comms feed her new reality. Her body was thrumming with residual exhaustion, but her focus was absolute: the long drive to Rico's asset transfer point outside Munich was their most exposed phase.

"Comms Lead, this is Rhys. Status holding. Current ETA to Rico's staging area is three hours, ten minutes," Rhys commanded, his voice tight from the sustained security watch. "Scarlett, confirm your systems check. We are maintaining absolute comms discipline."

Scarlett pressed the button to the comms unit, speaking low. "Comms Lead, LFO confirms stable. I'm running a full hardware diagnostic on the Ledger drive now. Status remains green." She was performing the required function, but the reality of their extreme operational poverty was setting in.

Her immediate concern was the physical asset identity she had used in Prague—Anastasia Radek. That profile was now burned, linked to the compliance drug protocol, the two neutralized security men, and the high-speed car chase. She dedicated the next hour to running triage on the "Anastasia Radek" persona. She killed the known email addresses, erased the fabricated social media accounts, and purged the initial purchase history of the red dress. The process was fast, efficient, and draining.

"Jacobs, I'm wiping the Radek ghost trail now," Scarlett reported, the action anchoring her in the strategic reality. "All known digital assets are being purged. No secondary trace vectors confirmed on this asset."

Arthur's voice was instantaneous, relief warring with tactical urgency. "Acknowledge, LFO. Good. But the physical asset remains the vulnerability. The unmarked vehicle is now associated with the Prague extraction. We need a confirmed plan for its disposal before you reach Munich."

"Rhys and Ben are planning an unsanctioned roadside transfer near the Munich staging area," Scarlett explained. "We move to Rico's vehicle on foot, leaving the Met asset on a secondary vector. We rely on Rico's expertise for the final disposal without leaving an institutional trace."

The Emotional Cost

She paused, placing the Ledger drive in her lap. The silence that followed was heavy with the weight of command. She was the Lead Field Operative, making life-and-life decisions, yet she missed the simple, domestic comfort of her husband's presence.

She initiated the private comms channel. "Arthur, tell me about Logan. Just... tell me something mundane."

Arthur's voice softened instantly, yielding to the partner. "Logan drew a picture of Jade and a very large, aggressive cat this morning. He tried to feed the satellite phone his breakfast. He's safe, Scarlett. He's oblivious, and he misses you. You focus on the extraction. I'm running secondary checks on the Mole's operational timing now."

The brief domestic anchor was a necessary shield. She had hours left of the drive. Hours of being the LFO, the strategist, the warrior. But she held onto the knowledge that she was also the partner, fighting for the quiet, chaotic safety of the life waiting for her.

Chapter 71: The Cost of Utility

The Logistical Emergency

The unmarked vehicle continued its relentless pace across the German autobahn, the low hum of the engine a constant drone. Hours had passed since Scarlett had wiped the "Anastasia Radek" persona, but she was still wearing the grim, uncomfortable remnants of her last mission: the heavy, drab blanket over the torn red silk dress.

"Comms Lead, this is Rhys. We are approximately one hour from the Munich staging area," Rhys announced over the comms. "We need to confirm the plan for the vehicle transfer and the physical asset acquisition."

Scarlett knew the next steps were critical, but a simple, overwhelming necessity was currently eclipsing strategic concerns. She pressed the comms button, overriding the operational chatter.

"Jacobs, before we finalize the transfer, I have a non-negotiable supply issue. I really need some different clothes. I left my knickers in Prague," Scarlett stated, forcing a light tone despite the seriousness of the underlying vulnerability.

The comms line went silent for a beat.

Then, Arthur's voice, laced with familiar exasperation and relief, filled her ear. "Scarlett! That is not a tactical priority! Your focus is asset security and visual checks! You are not stopping until Rico's perimeter is confirmed!"

"Acknowledge, Jacobs. But I am currently wearing a six-figure gown that is now unsalvageable and completely compromised," Scarlett countered, her voice hardening with her own frustration. "This isn't vanity; it's logistics. I need practical layers for the UK leg. Sweats, base layers, and utility wear. And underwear. Ben and Rhys cannot acquire these items without compromising their roles as perimeter security."

Arthur immediately shifted from furious husband to cold strategic commander. "Acknowledge, LFO. Tactical necessity confirmed. We cannot risk a roadside stop. Rhys, divert immediately to the *closest major service station*—high traffic, fast acquisition. Acquisition is strictly limited to utility wear—sweats, dark colors, and base layers. Cash purchase only. In and out in five minutes. Confirmed?"

Rhys sighed, the sound loud over the comms. "Understood, Comms Lead. Diverting to the next major service station. Acquisition team: Ben. Scarlett, you are restricted to the vehicle. You are too much of a liability in that dress."

The Briefest Respite

The service station was a chaotic blur of diesel fumes, neon lights, and hurried travelers. Scarlett, huddled low in the backseat, watched Ben—dressed in nondescript civilian clothes—run toward the convenience store with a wad of emergency cash. The five minutes felt like an hour.

When Ben returned, he efficiently tossed a large, nondescript bag into the backseat. "Acquisition complete. Dark sweats, a hoodie, thermal shirt, and, for God's sake, three packs of clean base layers. Change now. We lose five minutes of lead time, so we push the speed."

Scarlett gratefully pulled the privacy curtain. The silk dress was ruthless in its design; peeling it off felt like shedding a skin she never wanted to wear again. She quickly swapped the ruined glamour for the anonymous comfort of dark thermal wear and a plain hoodie. The weight of the new clothing—utility over vanity—felt like operational freedom.

"Comms Lead, LFO confirms identity swap. All high-value assets secured. I am now in a uniform appropriate for survival, not soft acquisition," Scarlett reported, tying the laces of the basic sneakers Ben had acquired.

"Acknowledge, LFO. Vector reassessment complete. Push speed to maximum limit. Munich ETA two hours, thirty minutes. You acquire Rico and disappear," Arthur commanded, his voice tight, the unsanctioned clothes a necessary, final cost.

Chapter 72: The Unsanctioned Rendezvous

The Final Approach

The interior of the unmarked vehicle was quiet now, the adrenaline of the initial escape having given way to a grim, focused exhaustion. The acquisition of utility wear had provided necessary physical relief; Scarlett was now clad in anonymous dark sweats and a hoodie, feeling the strange freedom of utility over glamour.

"Comms Lead, this is Rhys. Current ETA to the staging area is fifteen minutes," Rhys announced over the comms. "We'll be diverting onto the service road now. Ben, prep the handoff protocol."

Scarlett pressed the button to the comms unit. "Acknowledge, Rhys. LFO confirms transfer readiness. Jacobs, I need confirmation of Rico's visual marker. We run dark until we have eyes on the asset."

Arthur's voice, though sharp, was laced with an immense, palpable tension. "Acknowledge, LFO. Rico confirmed the marker. It will be a heavy-duty transport trailer, parked perpendicular to the road, with its hazard lights flashing once. He specializes in discretion, not visibility. That marker will disappear immediately after you confirm visual."

The vehicle began slowing, diverting onto a rough, unpaved service road outside the industrial sprawl of Munich. The air was cold, smelling of pine and diesel.

The Marker and the Hand-off

Rhys killed the headlights two minutes later. The only illumination came from the faint ambient glow of the distant city.

"Visual confirmed," Ben whispered from the passenger seat. "Heavy transport trailer, parked across the lane. Hazards are cycling. That's the marker."

The sight of the imposing, dark transport truck was a massive relief—and an immediate source of new dread. This was a clean line, but it was completely outside the protection of the Met.

"Comms Lead, LFO confirms marker sighting," Scarlett reported. "Ben and I dismount now. Rhys, initiate secondary exfil immediately after handoff. Do not wait."

"Understood, LFO. Good luck," Rhys confirmed, his voice thick with professional acknowledgment and personal apprehension.

Scarlett grabbed the secure transit case containing the Ledger drive. She pressed the comms button one last time. "Arthur, I'm going dark. You know the drill."

"I know, Scarlett. I'll be watching the perimeter. You acquire the transport and disappear. I love you."

She nodded, the gesture unnecessary, and slipped out of the vehicle with Ben. The transfer had to be instantaneous. She ran toward the transport trailer, her dark silhouette blending into the shadows.

A figure emerged from the cab—tall, heavily built, moving with a fluid, controlled stillness that immediately identified him as Arthur's former military equal. This was Rico.

"Anastasia?" Rico asked, his voice low and gruff, using the placeholder cover name.

"The name is Harper," Scarlett corrected instantly, bypassing the lie. "We're clean. We need the long run, Rico. You owe Arthur a marker."

Rico assessed the exhausted woman in sweats and the tense operative (Ben) in a single, devastating glance. He looked at the transit case in her hand. He didn't ask questions.

"The transport is prepped," Rico confirmed, his voice hard. "It runs dark. Ben, your Met vehicle is compromised. I'll dispose of it later. Get the LFO settled. We move in five minutes."

The New Ghost

The new transport—a heavy, soundproofed haulage vehicle—was a fortress. It was designed not just for transport, but for absolute operational discretion. It was stocked with basic rations, water, and—most importantly—a secure compartment containing the new set of high-grade identities.

Ben gave Scarlett a curt nod and disappeared back into the darkness to meet Rhys and initiate the secondary exfil. Scarlett was left alone with Rico, the last clean asset on the European continent.

The cost of the operation was clear: she was safe, but she was now permanently detached from the institutional protection of the Met. Her identity, her safety, and her path home were now entirely reliant on a single man's life debt to her husband.

Chapter 73: The Final Mandate

The Last Clean Line

The screens in the secure comms hub were dead. Arthur, the strategic command, was operating on raw, exhausting necessity, tethered to the digital world.

He accessed the secondary Met terminal to confirm the strategic information. The coordinates led to a small, private airstrip on the coast of Sicily. The file confirmed Gary's final asset liquidation target and extraction point.

Extraction Objective: Sicily. Ultimate destination: North Africa.

Arthur immediately initiated the emergency, unsanctioned line to Rico's rig.

"Rico, this is Jacobs. Urgent. Override destination. Sicily. Do you copy?"

Rico's voice, gruff and immediate, confirmed the change. "Acknowledge, Jacobs. Route override confirmed. Sicily it is. What's the price?"

"The price is done, Rico. Just keep her dark," Arthur managed, his voice thick with raw emotion.

He then sent one final, high-priority encrypted message to Deedee, coding the destination and the extraction point. His job was done. The strategic pieces were aligned.

The Ultimate Betrayal

The secure laptop began flashing violently. Deedee's emergency response protocol. Arthur opened the message, bracing himself for the institutional backlash.

He accessed it: a high-resolution, recent thermal image of Rico's massive transport trailer, parked discreetly outside the Munich industrial zone one hour after Rico had confirmed the handoff.

Superimposed over the heat signature of Rico's truck was a second, smaller, rapidly cooling thermal signature—a subtle, distinct pattern that spoke of recent, long-range surveillance. The Mole had moved to physical tracking of Rico's unsanctioned assets.

The file contained the final, damning piece of data: Metadata from the long-range thermal camera feed. The camera that captured the image was linked to a known Met unit—a specialist surveillance vehicle. Arthur cross-referenced the vehicle's log immediately.

The surveillance vehicle had been signed out 48 hours prior to the team crossing into Germany. The vehicle's designation: "Routine UK local security patrol." The sign-out officer: Rhys.

Arthur stared at the screen, every professional lesson he had ever learned crashing into the terrifying, visceral truth. Rhys was not the Mole, but his identity was the key used to betray the mission. The thermal camera, designed for high-value asset tracking, was deployed *under his credentials*.

The inescapable conclusion: the Mole had used Rhys's access codes—credentials necessary for his routine job vetting comms and vehicles—to deploy the physical tracking unit before the mission even began. The betrayal was rooted in Rhys's own job description and security permissions, making the framing absolute.

Arthur stared at the screen, the thermal image of Rico's truck burning into his retina. He was too late. He was trapped. And the Ledger, along with his wife, was heading directly into a fully compromised international pursuit, guided there by the very institutional access codes he had trusted.

He reached for the emergency satellite phone, not to call Deedee, but to send a final, cryptic warning to Rico. The long six months of remote vigilance had just become a terrifying game of cat and mouse with his own blood.

Printed in Dunstable, United Kingdom